Under The Meh-stletoe

A plus size holiday romance

Leonor Soliz

Leonor Soliz

Book Cover by Leonor Soliz

Illustrations by Leonor Soliz

First Edition

Ebook ISBN: 978-1-7380562-2-4

Paperback ISBN: 978-1-7380562-3-1

Contents

For all my holiday grouches.
We can survive the season together.

Author's Note

My books always end in a Happily Ever After. My stories are generally fluffy, with humor and light angst sprinkled in. Nevertheless, I believe it's important to give readers every chance to consent to reading my book. Although I write generally happy romance, if you'd like to access content warnings for this story, check **leonorsoliz.com/books/under-the-meh-stletoe**.

Join my newsletter

Have you received your copy of *Return To Love* yet? If not, make sure to join my newsletter and get a free friends-to-lovers, road trip novella.

Visit **leonorsoliz.com/newsletter** and join in the fun!

November 10

Ale

AS FAR AS LIFE-CHANGING events go, the breakup with my now-ex and my sister Renata's car accident fit the criteria. To top it off, things unfolded in such a way that I had been forced onto a Christmas committee as well. All in all, the end of the year was shaping up to be a complete nightmare.

The first committee meeting was scheduled to start in a couple of minutes, in the old community hall by the town's main square. I wrapped my fingers around the handle and willed myself to open the door. Instead, all I did was stare at it.

"Fuck. For Renata," I said, and swung the door open. It squeaked as it closed behind me.

Sure, I'd been the one to break up with my asshole boyfriend, and my twin sister had survived the car accident and would fully recover. Still, both events rocked me enough that they marked my life with a sharp before and after. After several years living in the city, it took me two weeks to pack up my stuff and return to the small town I grew up in, on the Northern Pacific coast. I even got bangs to mark the event.

The fact that I did so right at the start of the Christmas season had no relevance whatsoever. The small town of Laguna Island *loved* Christmas. I did not. It would be just my luck of late, that one thing led to another and now I would take my sister's place in the committee. It sucked.

"Ale!" Someone yelled as soon as I entered the room. The fact that they used the short version of my name and said it well, *Ah-leh*, settled warm in my stomach. "I can't believe you're back!"

Still, I had to fight to put a smile on my lips. It took a few seconds to place the voice and, after squinting at the person's face for a moment— a cool blonde bob curling around her jaw, big brown eyes with soft hints at wrinkles at the corners, and a huge smile— that I put it all together.

My grin turned real. "Janet?! Oh, wow!"

I strode through the community hall toward my high school classmate, ignoring the way the drab walls around the large space could use a new coat of paint. No decorations were up, letting the off-white— dirty white?!— show clearly. The tall rectangular windows didn't allow for much light to come in, and we were left to make do with cold, fluorescent tubes shining from the ceiling.

Janet stood by a makeshift table at the center of the room, lonely-looking with so much empty space surrounding it. Six raggedy chairs stood around it, in an old beige-gray combo that only added to the dull look of the space. I waved at the three other people sitting around the table, all of whom I'd met but didn't know well, and focused on my old friend. The petite blonde stood and opened her arms for a hug.

I walked into her embrace. "It's so good to see you! Why did we ever fall out of touch?"

"Because you moved away and I had three kids in quick succession," she laughed. "But I'm glad you're back. We need to go for coffee sometime! Eva opened this amazing place at the other side of the square, so we can let my kids tire themselves out while we catch up in peace. How long has it been? Ten years?"

"Eight," I said. "Only eight."

"That's eight years too long but, hey. Have one of these—"

Janet pushed a box toward me, already open and showing a selection of cookies. They were shaped in a Christmas theme and iced to look like colorful winter trees, sugar canes, and snowflakes.

Great. I didn't even like sweets, and now my friend looked at me like she expected me to squee in delight.

I was saved from having to taste a flour, sugar, and colorant snowflake and pretend like I had never enjoyed anything better, when a new figure entered the hall and stomped his way toward the center table.

"Six people. We're all here then. Let's start." His deep voice resounded in the space. His rushed steps echoed in the silence that followed.

With no hello, he sat down on one of the chairs and ruffled through his papers. Janet sat slowly and I mirrored her. No one uttered a word.

The man had curly dark hair and light brown skin. I didn't get to check the color of his eyes until he lifted his frown to the group and glared at us with dark brown irises. A deep wrinkle between his eyebrows marred his attractive face, his lips set in a tense line.

When his eyes settled on me, his frown deepened. "You're not Renata."

His tone was so grumpy that it made me want to make fun of him. I didn't, if only because I didn't know him, and didn't know if he could take it graciously.

"Maybe the car accident made me change my style." The sarcasm imbued in my words was unplanned.

While we obviously had extremely similar looks, Renata kept her natural brown hair color, while the bottom half of mine was dyed in shades of pink and orange ombre. I also wore dark green cat-eye glasses while she wore contacts, and I wore lots of black and pleather while she loved colorful clothing.

She had also been in a scary car accident and was in the middle of recovery. She couldn't volunteer for the Christmas committee like she did every year and had begged me to rush my return so I could take her place.

He squinted at me. "Identical twins, then. It's fine, as long as we get the extra hands. You'll do."

He went back to his paperwork, effectively dismissing me. A mix of pride and irritation rumbled in my stomach. My nostrils flared. Now I didn't care if he couldn't take me making fun of him. I would have a blast despite him.

I smirked.

"Daniel—" Janet cleared her throat— "Daniel, this is Alejandra. She just came back to Laguna Island a few days ago."

Barely contained exasperation seemed to exude from his every pore.

He took what seemed like a long-suffering, calming breath and left his papers on the table. "And I was voluntold to be the Town's point of contact and local government representative for the Christmas season celebrations. Let's do that, okay? We all know each other, or we will get to over the next six weeks. This town does way too much for the holidays and we just need to survive it. You'll be the president, Alejandra."

I laughed. "No, I won't be."

He cast his eyes at me again. "I was told that your sister was always the president, wasn't she?"

Yes, but that was because even though we had the exact same genetic material, somehow, she loved Christmas with a passion while I couldn't stand it.

"I'm only here for my sister," I said. "I don't want to be the president. Can't we cast a vote or something?"

"Come on," Janet said. The other volunteers around the table stared at their laps and seemed inclined to let the chips fall where they may. Even Pri, who I'd met because she was Renata's best friend, pretended the plastic surface between us was fascinating. "You can get Ren to provide moral support and her extensive knowledge. With her by your side, you'll do a much better job than any of us could."

"What about you?" I asked her. "You love Christmas, don't you?"

"I do! Very much. What's not to love? Yummy foods, there's cozy music everywhere, everyone smiles—" she stole a glance at Daniel— "or almost everyone. I get to make cookies and do crafts, and to have an excuse to leave my kids with their grandma for longer. It's my break, you know? Same with all of them." She pointed at the other three people around us. "And we have a blast with it."

"Then one of you should be the president! You love this stuff."

"Don't you love Christmas?"

"I don't love it, no. I'm… neutral." I bit my tongue not to explain that it was gross optimism, to say I was neutral about it. "So I'm not the right person for it."

"We can't do it," Janet started at the same time as Daniel spoke up, and she quieted to let him take over.

"You'll be perfect then." He held my gaze. "This bunch can't do it. They blow the budget every time, all in the spirit of the holidays, according to the briefing I received. Renata was the first to corral them into shape. The town was about to cancel the celebrations altogether due to lack of funding."

"She organized the fundraising and kept us to budget." Janet stared at the other three people at the table, asking for silent support— she got it in the form of energetic nods.

I did my best to ignore the fact that the accident had happened on my sister's drive back from a fundraising event.

"I see." It was my turn to frown. "So my disinterest actually protects the celebrations. Ren didn't tell me I'd have to preside the committee when she begged me to come in her name."

"Welcome to the party." Daniel's words were laced with the same lack of joy I felt. "We're co-chairs now. We'll exchange phone numbers before we leave so we can reach out to each other in case of a seasonal emergency."

"Seasonal emergency?" I scoffed, then had to suppress a smile when I imagined an ambulance playing Christmas music instead of a siren. "What kind of things does the town do these days for Christmas?!"

"Decorations for Main Street," Janet listed with a finger, followed by the rest as she went on. "My favorite, the cookie decoration competition; Letters to Santa, which is our gift donation drive; the Christmas car parade; and of course, the big community Christmas party right here, for which we have to decorate as well. It's not too much, and we have so much fun!"

I held back a groan. This sounded dreadful to me. "Great. And as president, I will have to do what, exactly?"

"Be my point of contact." Daniel didn't sound happy about it. "Organize all the volunteers, about fifty total, and keep them to task. I'll do that too. Keep the morale high and such. Make sure we have all the supplies we need. And of course, put out any fires."

"Wonderful." Sarcasm dripped from the word. "Keeping the morale high for Christmas sounds *exactly* like my jam. Just wonderful."

"We will all help." Janet rubbed my shoulder in an encouraging manner that did nothing to make me feel better. "You won't do it alone. It's the season of joy, isn't it? A cookie will make it better."

She pushed the box in my direction. I picked the smallest cookie I could see and forced a minimal bite into my mouth.

I hoped she wouldn't see the resulting grimace.

———

The air had that crisp combined smell of winter and beach that I remembered so well, as I walked back to Renata's and my house. My feet still knew the streets of my youth, allowing me to admire the little changes that had appeared over the years. Maybe a house had changed color, or flowers had become bushier and fuller. Beyond that, things seemed to be the same, and it warmed me up from within. It helped push away the feeling left behind after the meeting, and I smiled.

It had taken only eight weeks, but my life changed twice in as many months. First, my dickhead of an ex changed his mind a hundred times about our future, and full-on panicked when I said my lease was coming up and I wanted to buy a house. I broke up with him, licked my wounds, and started looking for options.

Three weeks later and at two in the morning, my dad called me from Perú to tell me Ren was in the hospital. I moved heaven and earth to make it to her and, as soon as she was stable enough for us to know she would make it, I'd started the process of returning to Laguna Island. Now we lived together, and we focused on putting our lives back in order— me metaphorically, and her almost literally. At least, thanks to her insurance and all my savings during my accountant career, we were in no rush.

I sighed as I reached our childhood home. Ren moved into it after Dad had left to live back home with his wife. My sister had made it her own; she slept in the principal room, while I slept in what had been our bedroom growing up. The keys clinked as I opened the main door, and I stepped right into the living room.

It still shocked me that the wall that used to separate the kitchen from the dining space was gone. An island now divided the two areas, overlooking the table and its four chairs, and the living room. The décor was mostly the same, with furniture that used to be modern in the 90s, and a few new paintings that gave the whole house an eclectic flair that suited my sister well. They fit nicely with the print of Incan textile art I'd grown up admiring, still the focus of the room.

Ren appeared to have been napping on the sofa, still sitting up like she hadn't meant to fall asleep, with a blanket keeping her warm. She opened her eyes when I came inside, but she looked exhausted, like she could easily pass out again. She'd lost weight while in the hospital and her clothes didn't fit her as well; there was still a paleness to her. It made my heart ache.

"Stop looking at me like that," she said. "I'm okay."

I sat next to her on the sofa. "You *will* be okay."

"I'm recovering nicely. I may still be bruised... may still have stitches in organs I'd rather not think about... I may fall asleep ten times a day..." She groaned as she adjusted on the couch to sit up better. "But I'm okay."

A wave of gratefulness that my sister was still alive coursed through me. I hooked my arm around hers and put my head on her shoulder.

"How was the first meeting? I love the excitement everyone feels for it." Her voice sounded rough, but more awake.

Since she couldn't see me, I rolled my eyes. Janet and the rest may have been bright-eyed as we discussed all the tasks, but I wasn't. Daniel hadn't been either, for that matter.

I sighed. "I'm going to need your help. I have no idea what I'm doing."

"I'm sorry I can only offer my brain right now, and only when I'm not napping. Everything else still hurts."

"Of course! Don't worry. I just need to know what to do. There are way too many things to be done, and half the people in town are too busy wanting to know where I've been for the past few years to let me do anything."

I had tried to run a few errands after the meeting but gave up right away. People kept inviting me for a drink and chatting me up, slowing me down. If I didn't find a way to keep a good pace without insulting everyone, I'd never be free from this committee nightmare.

"Maybe you can use it as a chance to reconnect with everyone? You're back but you've been mostly here at home keeping me company. The committee could be good for you."

"Yeah, yeah. That's what you said as part of your speech to get me to do this Christmas thing for you. That I can take it as an opportunity to sow seeds, and the next few weeks to grow roots again here. Would you like something to drink?"

"A tea sounds good."

I got up and went straight for the kettle.

"I still believe what I told you, by the way," Ren continued. "You left and then didn't stay in touch with lots of people. If you spend time with everyone again, they'll be happy with you. They'll welcome you back, and they'll want to help you."

I set two mugs on the island and put a teaspoon of sugar in each. "You make it sound like I need to pay penance for being gone for eight years."

"Not quite that but... somewhat."

"Fine. I'll do my best."

The water boiled, and I added teabags and water to the mugs.

"Great." Ren pushed herself higher on the sofa and, though she tried to hide a grimace, I saw it in her features. "So tell me— who's helping from the Town? It can make such a difference."

Nope, my heart hadn't recovered yet from seeing her in pain. If she didn't want to show it, then I wouldn't bring it up again.

"Daniel," I responded. "No one told me his last name, but he's cranky? Has great curls but also frowns a lot?"

I stirred the drinks and brought the mugs to the living room. Ren made room for me next to her, lifting the blanket around her to invite me for a mini fort. It was something we used to do as children, share a blanket as we sat on the sofa, and doing it again sparked warmth in me.

"I know who Daniel is. Attractive but grumpy. He got here like a year ago and hit the ground running trying to prettify the town. He thinks we can be a tourist destination."

I arched an eyebrow. "I mean, I agree. We could be..."

"If we had the money for it, yeah. Most of the town is letting him try but... I don't know if that'll work out."

We sat next to each other, shoulder to shoulder, warm drinks in our hands.

"Do you think that he's cranky *and* stubborn? Will he stay if he can't make it happen, do you think?"

Ren cut a glance at me. "Why, are you interested?"

"What? No." I shook my head. "He looks good, but I'm done with grumps."

She laughed. "You like grumps. You're great with grumps. They love you. And you won't be able to help yourself. You'll try to make him laugh and think it's a personal win."

"Uh-uh. I'm so done. Vincent was my last."

I sipped from my tea and hoped Ren would drop it. She didn't.

"Vincent wasn't simply grumpy. He was flakey."

"True. It doesn't mean I'm on the lookout for someone else."

"I don't know. It could be a Christmas miracle."

I laughed. "Please. Do not. If you think Daniel is a Christmas romance hero, you're welcome to him."

"Me? I don't like grumps, and I can hardly seduce him in my current state."

"You could seduce anyone you liked at any point—"

"And I might do that one day, but not Daniel. So if you wanted to see where that could go..."

"Stop. I want to be single for a season at least. Okay? And I'll be too busy organizing all these Christmas events to seduce anyone. I asked because of the future of the town, not because of him. Now let me do my best to get into the Christmas spirit. I'm going to need all the help I can get."

November 17

Daniel

A WEEK AFTER THE first committee meeting, I entered the community hall we used as planning headquarters, a frown knotting my eyebrows. Boxes of past years' decorations littered the place, while the committee inspected every piece of tinsel and fake branch of mistletoe.

The frown stayed firmly in place as I sat at the table with my clipboard in hand. Biting my tongue didn't come naturally to me. If I thought something and believed I was right, I said it. Despite my natural tendencies to speak my mind, when I was told to be the Town's liaison for the community party committee, I kept my opposition to the role in the privacy of my mind. For one reason and one reason only— it would serve my goal to keep the community Christmas party going. No matter how much I despised the season, protecting the celebrations meant guarding the small-town spirit.

From my chair, I surveyed the group and checked off items on my list. Finalize committee set up— check. Determine decorating team— check. I'd sent the email an hour before. Choose a committee president— check.

I pursed my lips and searched for Ale from my vintage point. Being familiar with Renata didn't prepare me for the shock of a very similar face surrounded by fun-colored hair, and an alluring body dressed in way cooler clothes. Glasses that made her eyes stand out in the prettiest way, and curves that demanded attention and promised handfuls of soft flesh everywhere. Really inconvenient, to notice the reaction that such simple changes caused in me.

It couldn't matter. I had to be neutral. Even if her long, sharp, dark green nails promised to beckon me and take me to my knees.

Impartiality had to be my middle name.

"Alejandra," I called. "Can we talk for a sec?"

My conflicted thoughts must have shown on my face, because Alejandra squinted at me as if questioning my intentions. I raised an eyebrow, daring. That's what I would have done with anybody else. Ale wouldn't get preferential treatment.

She'd been checking a string of LED lights for failing bulbs, and she left it on top of a box.

She leaned against the table, the generous line of her hip against it. "Yeah? Everything okay?"

"Not going to be okay until New Year's Eve in my opinion, but since I can't skip Christmas, it's pointless to go there." I let my voice drip with the scorn I felt for the holidays. "I still need to check-in about a few things with the committee's president."

Humor shone in her eyes, and her lips curled in a tiny, mostly hidden smile.

"That wasn't funny. Why are you smiling?" I asked.

"I'm not smiling. See?" She frowned, but the upward tilt of her lips intensified. "I'm very serious."

"I thought you didn't like Christmas either, the way you talked about it last week."

"Anyway." She ignored my comment and sat on the chair next to me. "What did you want to talk about?"

The impulse to insist on an answer pushed through me, but I bit it back.

I glued my eyes to my clipboard. "I called the extended volunteer team and coordinated with the Town's services. Decoration of Main Street should happen next week as planned."

I would rock this neutrality thing.

"Wonderful." Her tone contradicted her statement. "Would you consider vandalism on the decorations?"

A chuckle wanted to escape me, but I trapped it inside. If I found her funny we might end up connecting, and I wasn't here to connect with any one particular person. I was here to be fucking Switzerland. I'd be casual acquaintances with everyone in equal measure, and no one in particular.

"Any news on the gift giving extravaganza?" I asked.

She shook the foot she kept over her knee, the same little smirk on her lips. "I talked to the school; they'll have the teachers drop hints. I also talked to the librarians, the post office, and the Town's community support workers. We should have a bunch of kids sending letters to Santa soon. I'm still organizing the matching of donors with letters."

"What about Santa himself? Have you talked to him yet?"

"Nope. I delegated that task to Janet."

"You... delegated?" A tiny little smile of my own put pressure on my mouth, and I wasn't fast enough to prevent it this time. "It used to be your sister's task."

"Absolutely, and I delegated it. Privileges of the president." She leaned forward to me and, shielding her lips from everyone else's view— their loss, as the shape of her full mouth, close like this— it was charming. She whispered, "It works because it's less Christmas nonsense on my to-do list."

I chuckled. She winked.

"We're kindred spirits on this then." I frowned at my own admittance. This could be a slippery slope. Better cut it short. "But that's not the point."

"The point is I made you laugh!"

"Not the point, and it was a snort at best."

"I consider it my good deed for the season."

"That's really poor marketing for your personal brand. Your good deed should be volunteering for this committee."

No one around us seemed to be paying close attention to Ale's shenanigans. I released a measured gust of air. Everyone continued to organize decorations into piles and chat among themselves. Good.

My future did not include a house on the suburbs or a white picket fence. I wanted a simple life, where people in town liked me enough to drink a beer with me, and then let me go when I'd met my social quota and wanted to go home.

I didn't need to focus on a partner to get community. Relationships were rarely worth the effort, and I was comfortable on my own. Even if a spark spluttered in my gut in response to Ale, I wouldn't fan it.

"In the season of joy, I promise I won't let anybody know that you're capable of chuckling," Ale said.

I don't know what I showed on my face, but it made her grin. It was a beautiful smile.

I tore my eyes away. "You can go right ahead and tell everyone that I chuckled. I'm known to laugh once in a while. In any case— party planning."

She let me divert our conversation, though that teasing gleam in her eyes remained. I ignored it. If Costa Rica could make away with its military forces because they were so neutral, so damn peaceful, so could I.

Moving to Laguna Island was a critical step in my life plans. Within three years, I hoped to set up a comfortable life in a strong-knit community. Unattached and free. Reconnected to my Latine roots, mostly invisible to me beyond my last name and my parents' ethnicity, and at peace.

When I studied the history of Laguna Island, I learned that over the seventies and eighties, a big wave of immigrants had settled in what then was a mostly abandoned town. A number of these newcomers were refugees from Latin America, and that's when the town had changed its name and embraced a multicultural, melting pot vision.

Soon word spread among immigrants, especially those coming from Central and South America, that this slice of land on the North Pacific coast welcomed people who left their home abroad.

Immigrants found comfort in coming together with people who understood, really understood, what that meant. They made a third culture together. Not fully here, not ever back there, but with each other.

I wanted some of that. The vision was clear. I would find a way to bring money into the town and earn my place among the Laguninos.

Sparkly eyes, intriguing humor, and an attractive body would not make me sway.

November 24

Ale

SEVERAL DAYS HAD GONE by since the last committee meeting, and every one of those days had been filled to the brim with errands and tasks. That afternoon was the first day in a long time when I could sit and chill with Ren at home. My sister and I sat on the sofa and shared a blanket once more; she read a book while I watched a movie. It brought a cozy feeling to the familiar old living room, like we were teenagers again. In the warmth of our cocoon, I could pretend I hadn't almost lost my twin, and we had a bright future ahead.

I bit the inside of my mouth. At least we likely had a bright future ahead. She'd fully recover and go back to her job at the library, and I'd come up with something to do with my life now that I was back in my hometown.

Maybe I'd ask Eva if she had any leads. If she didn't, I'd ask Renata. When she felt better.

I'd watched the film lighting up the screen several times, and the next bit was one of my favorites.

I elbowed my sister. "Look! The pool scene is happening."

Renata put a finger on her page and lifted her eyes to the TV. We both admired the way the actor pulled himself out of the water, drops and rivulets falling down his skin, his bright green eyes staring right at us.

We sighed in unison.

"That man is way too perfect." Renata went back to her book.

I smirked. She was right, but it didn't mean we didn't enjoy the sight.

"Did you know he's married to a Latina filmmaker? To think that could have been one of us."

She chuckled. "Since when did you plan to become a movie director?"

"Since I heard you could catch a man like that."

"Ha, so you *are* looking for romance."

I didn't respond. From the corner of my eye, I caught my phone lighting up with an incoming text. I checked it without giving it much thought. The next scene in the movie was with the antagonist, and I didn't care much for it.

Regret hit me almost instantly when I read the message.

"Fuck," I muttered.

"What?" Renata lifted her eyes at me, a finger marking her spot on the page again.

"There's no Santa."

For a moment, she didn't respond. She simply stared at me.

I turned my phone and showed her the text I'd received from Janet.

> **Janet**: Don Nicolás, the guy that was our Santa for years, is gone. He moved to the City to live with his son. What do we do?!

"Don Nicolás moved?!" Renata asked. "When?! How?! I can't believe we didn't know!"

I may not have lived in Laguna Island for the last eight years, but I hadn't forgotten how to translate that. In such a small town, losing a community member without notice was a rare occurrence.

"Big mystery, I'm sure." I started a text message on my phone. "But I'm going to assume this is a huge problem?"

> **Ale**: apparently there's no Santa

I sent the text to Daniel and went back to my sister.

"Hell yes, it's a huge problem," she said. "Santa *makes* the cookie decoration competition! The kids ask for him! They line up to take pictures with him. And I can't imagine the big party without him. No. Ale. This can't be."

The panic that settled in her eyes told me everything I needed to know.

"It's okay." I rubbed her shoulder in what I hoped was a soothing gesture. I wasn't sure; comfort came naturally to me in most situations, but not when the words building on my tongue were, *relax, who cares? It's just a guy in a red suit.* "Ren, it's okay."

"But we need to find someone! Right away. We don't have enough time! We might have to pick someone without a beard.

No. No. Ale. We can't put someone in a fake, plastic, white beard. What if a kid *pulls* it?!"

Not a big deal.

But she blanched, so I pushed the thought down. "I'll get a high-quality beard, I promise. We'll glue it on if we need to."

I checked my phone. No answer from Daniel.

"But for whom?" she continued. "We might need to reach out to people living in acreages. Far away ones—"

Was she scared because of her accident? Was the idea of traveling long distances scary to her these days?

"I'll get Daniel to take me if I need to." I took her hand and squeezed. "We're good."

Still no text from him, though.

"I'll have to go through my list of backup Santas," she said. "You can go beg them to volunteer."

"Now we're talking. That's an actionable plan. Why don't you send me the list?"

"I'll write it up while you go find Daniel. Then I'll text it to you."

"What? Why do I need to go find Daniel?"

"He needs to know there's an emergency. He could have access to resources we don't, like lists of people and their ages and locations—"

"Sooo... I'm not finding him to ask him to dress up like Santa?" I entertained the image for a glorious second. It made me laugh.

"No! He's too young. And too hot."

Well, that he was. I didn't entertain *that* thought for long.

"He's too grumpy, too." I frowned. "Isn't Santa supposed to be smiling all the time?"

"That too! So, no. You could pester him about calling the police department and ask them to run a search for folk of the right age—"

You've got to be kidding me. A police search?

"It's not that serious," I interrupted. "Is it?"

"It's only a month until Christmas. Yes, it's that serious. Things move faster than you think, preparing for the season. We're supposed to make miracles happen!"

I barely held back from rolling my eyes. If miracles happened, they could happen at any time of the year. Or Halloween, maybe; that was a holiday that whispered magic. Christmas? It was a season of toxic positivity, in my opinion.

But my sister loved it, so I didn't say much.

"I know you're indifferent to the holidays." She put her free hand on top of mine, forming a tower of comforting hand squeezing.

I stared at it. It was okay if she believed I was indifferent to Christmas; it was better than her finding out it annoyed me to no end.

She continued, "I'm already so so so thankful you're taking over the organization of all the events. That you're running things for me."

"Of course. I'd do anything for you." And that was true.

"I know." She smiled, the gesture sweet. It gave me a heart pang, in thankfulness I still got to see it. "And I love you as much as always for it. And..."

I chuckled. I had a pretty good idea of what would come next. "And?"

"And I would really appreciate it if you found it in your heart to search for Daniel and get the ball rolling on this. We can't not have a Santa."

Her eyes shone with hope as she waited for an answer. Since my dad's call a few weeks ago, I had gained a new sense of responsibility over her. It trickled down my chest, heavy and warm in equal measure. I had promised myself I'd do anything while she recovered. I could do this to make her happy.

"Fine." I sighed and reached for my phone. "I'll get the ball rolling."

Ale: SOS WE HAVE NO SANTA

I sent Daniel the follow up text. Even though I glared at the screen, the three dots failed to make an appearance.

"Would you consider going to the Town Hall and tracking him down?" Renata put her bookmark in place and tucked her novel between her leg and the sofa arm. "Then you could start the search for Santa right away."

"This *must* be the plot of a film somewhere, right?"

The movie I'd been watching, which had no reference to Christmas whatsoever, continued to play on the TV. We missed the scene of the hero stripping for the heroine, but I didn't complain. Apparently, we were dealing with an urgent matter.

"What, like a holiday romcom?" She grinned. "The heroine is forced to spend time with the hero, and they slowly fall in love."

My laughter exploded. "No way. No, I meant more like, one of those with life lessons, based on an old fairytale, which was subverted to have a happy ending it was never meant to have."

"Wow." She laughed too. "Where did all that bitter come from?"

With Christmas? It comes from deep in my soul.

But I laughed it off, put on my jacket, and made my way to the Town Hall.

Daniel

Ropes— check.

Hooks— check.

Netting— check.

Work gloves— check.

Ax—

I smiled. Anticipation over using the tool with as much strength as I could summon coursed through me.

Check.

The cherry on top was that, instead of my usual standard pickup truck, I got to use the one main service truck the town owned. I closed the toolbox tucked in the back, and secured the small pulley system that would help me bring back a big-enough tree. My intention was to get behind the wheel as fast as possible and drive into the hills, but Ale intercepted me before I could.

She approached me with purpose, hands deep in her leather jacket. Her black jeans hugged her wide hips, while a deep purple hoodie peeked through her collar; it contrasted with the pinks and oranges of her hair. Her eyebrows furrowed, and the sight sparkled inside me in recognition.

She was a little snarky, I was cranky, and I liked the combination.

Except I didn't. Not at all. Or at least, I didn't mean to like it.

"Hey," she said. "Did you see my text?"

She stopped a short distance from me, my back to the truck. We stood alone in the parking lot, dense clouds heavy above us. Her eyes were the only thing that glittered in the diffuse light shining on us.

I would think about it, probably right before I feel asleep.

I cleared my throat. "My phone is somewhere in the truck's cab. So... no."

I rubbed my hands together. It was a cold day; I shifted in my spot to warm myself up and release some of my nervous energy.

She raised an eyebrow, a small smirk tilting her lips. "I texted you an hour ago."

"Sure. I haven't touched my phone in a few hours. Did you need me for something?"

"There's a seasonal emergency. Santa's missing." She crossed her arms.

I groaned and shut my eyes. "Fun."

"Loads."

I took a deep breath. We would need to discuss details, brainstorm some options. I could either go back to my tiny office, postponing the tree cutting, or postpone the conversation.

"I'll text you in a few hours," I said.

"Oh, no. I don't trust that, considering the response to my latest."

"Email me. I'll respond tonight."

She gave me a friendly punch on the arm. "C'mon. Give me five minutes to talk about this. I only need the simplest of plans... or the next two steps."

I squinted at her. She grinned. It did exactly what I imagined she expected. My resolve melted several degrees.

Ale dipped her head in the direction of the town hall, as if motivating me to go back in there for a few minutes. She stared at me with an innocent look. A reticent smirk twisted the corner of my mouth.

"Five minutes," she insisted.

If Ale had returned to Laguna Island to stay, I might as well get used to having her in my vicinity. Avoiding her wouldn't work, anyway. In fact, if we spent more time together, this pesky little spark of attraction might run its course and go to the land where all infatuations went to die.

"Fine. You have two hours." I opened the passenger's door. "Get in the truck."

"Excuse me?"

"Please," I added, in case that was her issue. "We'll talk on the way there."

It worked. She got in the truck, while I rounded the front and got in the driver's seat.

"Where are we going?" She latched her seatbelt to its closure.

I did the same and started the motor. "We're going for a tree."

"A… Christmas one, perhaps?"

"The only highlight of the damn season. I get to chop down a tree."

And vent all my frustrations into it.

We left the parking lot and I drove toward the outskirts of the town. I turned on the local radio station, and its old, recorded programming filled the cab. In the year I'd lived in Laguna Island, I had learned the whole repertoire. By this point, I knew what the next three songs would be.

"Wow. That sounds like my childhood." Ale sighed. "Why are you listening to that?"

"It makes me feel like a local."

And the next song would be one of my favorites by Soda Stereo, and I didn't want to miss out on it.

She laughed. "No local listens to the local radio station. We're in the age of streaming, did you know?"

"I do that at home but thank you for caring about the quality of my musical enrichment."

"Pfft, please. What I care about is why we're going to chop down a tree. I know we have millions of those around but cutting one down sounds so anti-environment."

We neared the urban edges of Laguna Island. I took the road toward the hills, and ancient forests immediately surrounded us. Soon I'd get to smell wood and dirt and leaves and, after I put all my strength into chopping down the tree, I'd feel as relaxed as I'd ever been.

Couldn't wait. I just needed to pretend that having Ale around didn't change anything.

I kept my eyes on the road, instead of stealing a glance at her like I wanted to. "Real trees for Christmas are more ecological than buying plastic, if that's what you're thinking."

"That's exactly what I'm thinking."

Driving was easy in Laguna Island. Traffic was non-existent, and we breezed down the street at a constant speed. The conifer forest was dense around us, deep green under the gray clouds.

I shook my head. "The town has a plot of land in the hills reserved for this purpose. This is the *most* ecological way to do it. Do you have any idea the levels of carbon emissions that go into making plastic ones?"

"Okay, fine. I get it. I'm sure it's not even about wanting to feel all brawny in the process. You do it for the climate, right?"

I broke and stole a glance at her. "If someone cuts down a tree and no one's there to see it happen, was the person brawny at all?"

"What are you talking about?"

"Like that saying. If a tree falls, did it make a sound?" I turned the truck to a side road, the forest even closer at our sides.

"That never made sense to me." Ale huffed. "Anyway, we should talk about Santa. I've been informed this is a big deal."

"Maybe it's a good thing, actually. Santa is so damn creepy. Such a blatant way to manipulate kids. Behave, children, or else there will be no joy for you."

She slapped her thigh with vehemence. "You're singing the song of my people! Can you imagine the first person to come up with it? So evil. Let's scare the kids into doing what I want. Let's teach them there's someone watching... and judging."

"Exactly."

"But my sister said that Santa is critical to the competitions and the big party. She implied kids will be sad without him."

"I can see the town council being upset."

The road turned to gravel, and it narrowed down further. Soon we'd be going up, until the road became little more than a walking path.

"I guess we can't have it our way." She squirmed in her seat, reaching toward her generous rear with a hand. The curving lines of her ass were so squeezable that I had to grasp the wheel for dear life, not to reach and pinch the tempting expanse of flesh.

From the corner of my eye— dammit, if I could keep my attention away from her— I watched her scroll on her phone.

She fixed her glasses. "Good news, my sister sent me a list of people she thinks we should approach for help. What's your email address? I'll send it to you."

We dealt with that, agreed that she'd reach out to them by phone and provide a summary to me by email, and switched to discussing the rest of the tasks we oversaw.

"City decoration on the weekend, then?" she asked.

"Yep. The big team will be there. The lighting of the tree still scheduled for Wednesday night?"

"Depends on whether we have a tree by then, I guess."

"Ha. We will. Never thought to ask about that, did you?"

"If it's not on my committee to-do list, I won't notice. Believe it or not, I don't spend a lot of time thinking about what makes a proper Christmas..."

And I liked that about her... a little. Never a lot.

Ale

Despite growing up in Laguna Island and living here for the first twenty years of my life, I had never been up this road before.

Daniel parked the very end of a path. I followed him through a trail I couldn't see, surrounded by old trees; a patchwork of moss and old growth spotted the ground and wrinkly trunks. The smell of it was glorious and I filled my lungs with it. I'd missed it while in the City, nearly as much as I'd missed the ocean. Not because I was too far from it or couldn't come visit, but because it meant so much to me. It hit different at home.

"Are you sure you don't want to stay in the truck?" Daniel asked. He carried gloves and an ax. "It's warm there."

"I don't mind the cold, but I mind having to stay there alone. What if I get abducted by aliens? You'd be tried for murder, sir."

One of my boots slid in a mix of mud and wet leaves, but I didn't mind. At least I wouldn't get creeped out by having no one around and no phone signal. Having to pull the arborist dolly behind me was a minor inconvenience.

"Maybe you're too used to city living," Daniel said.

"Yeah, I got used to it. Sue me. But I still remember all of this." I sighed. "I still love it. Though I wouldn't have come back yet, if it weren't for Ren's accident."

We reached a clearing where perhaps a hundred pine trees in different stages of growth lined up in perfect rows, evenly distributed.

"Daniel Cabrera. Did you do this?"

I had learned in the past couple of weeks that he'd been hired as the Public Works Director, and as such he'd focused on all sort of projects to better the town. Many of the trees looked too big for his influence after only a year, but the amazement escaped me anyway. Perhaps he was that good.

He snorted. "No. This was one of the few great ideas my predecessor had. I just get to reap the rewards."

He stopped by a nicely shaped pine tree, probably over fifteen feet high. He dropped the ax to the ground and inspected the trunk. I stayed several steps away.

"I heard about her accident," he added. "Impossible not to, in a small town. I'm glad she's okay."

"Me, too. I wish she were feeling better, both for her sake and mine— then she'd be the one helping you out. She'd be much better than I am."

It was cold. Our breaths turned into vapor with each word we uttered. He looked up to the tip of the pine tree, and my eyes kept on going up the sightline. Clouds still covered the sky, but it didn't look like rain.

"You're doing fine." He studied the canopy. "Just up the cranky and we'll be perfect."

I spluttered. "What cranky?"

He slapped the trunk of the tree for a mysterious reason. He stole a glance at me. "Fine. Let's call it snark."

I wanted to be offended. Even if he was right. Never mind the fact I had just suggested he might be tried for murder.

I crossed my arms. "You mean the sarcasm? Or the humor I add to my words? You know how to recognize humor, right?"

Sure, if I were a better person, I'd admit sarcasm only made ten percent of my comments, and that I tended to joke things away, so we didn't have to go too deep into anything. But that was absolutely beside the point. I just didn't want him to call it crankiness.

I must have made a gesture with my face because he chuckled. It was a dark sound. He cleared a few of the lower branches with quick and precise swings of the ax.

"I have a list and checked it twice, Ale. Every time we've met, I've seen a pesky little spark in your eyes. You call it sarcasm; I call it *an attitude*."

"Har har." I ignored the fact it sounded like he'd been paying attention to my eyes. "What if the snark is just my attitude around you? Maybe I'm a ray of sunshine with everyone else."

"Maybe it's me, you mean?" He dropped the ax on the ground again and strolled to me, casual as he unzipped his jacket. My logical mind must have been too busy keeping track of the bickering to stop my body from reacting, because the sight caught my breath. My eyes followed his hand as he pulled the tab down, the sound of tiny metal teeth unclasping filling the space between us.

My face warmed. He took off his jacket. I gulped. His buttoned-up shirt was plaid, of fucking course, in shades of blue and green. It made his dark hair stand out and it showcased the shape of him. The triangle of his torso, and the cutest little tummy. Cuddling him would feel cozy in all the best ways. Not that I would consider cuddling with him. Or anyone, really.

He stared at me, challenging, and with another tiny smirk on his lips. "I don't know. Somehow, I doubt it. I'd bet you're snarky with everyone."

He pushed his jacket toward me; I pursed my lips and took it. We held each other's eyes as he warmed up muscles and joints.

He moved his arms and shoulders in wide circles, and lifted his legs in high marching motions. He finally twisted at the waist a few times, all the while sporting a teasing twinkle in his eyes.

"Apparently I'm not the only one capable of snark," I said.

"Isn't it interesting, how many people confuse it with being a grump?" He went back to the tree and put on the working gloves he'd dropped to the ground, giving me a nice view of his ass.

Not that I had meant to look. It just had been... there. The fact it had turned out to be an attractive sight was secondary.

I took a deep breath, with the intention to anchor myself to the ground again rather than fall prey to whatever my hormones were doing. I failed. A whiff of smell reached me from his jacket and my attention zeroed in on it, wanting more. I bit back a groan; everything seemed to be going sideways during this short outdoorsy adventure.

He didn't wait for my response. He grabbed the ax, swung it a few times to further warm up his muscles, and started on a rant instead.

"It's like everyone else in this town." With no warning, he swung the ax at the trunk in front of him. The whole tree shivered, and so did I. "I chose Laguna Island carefully—" he pulled the ax back and swung it again, letting out a groan— "the state of the town meant great housing options— " he released the ax, huffed, and swung again— "and great long-term affordability."

He repeated the motion, freeing the ax, swinging it again, and grunting. The tree continued to tremble, my legs continued to weaken, and he continued his tirade amid all his hard breathing.

Seemed competence porn was a turn on these days for me. I bit my lip and hoped for a reprieve.

"I get to Laguna Island... a shiny new job... that would let me grow roots... while helping strengthen... a better future... for all of us... only to discover... the town is... in worse shape... than I thought."

No reprieve in sight. His wide shoulders, strong chest, and thick thighs made everything worse. The sounds he made went straight to my lower belly; it seemed that an attractive man going full lumberjack had me all hot and bothered. I wasn't pleased about it. I was soooo not interested. So done with grumps!

He kept hacking at the tree in a hypnotizing rhythm. "So who cares..." Grunt. "If I'm a little cranky..." Hard breathing. "Because getting the town in order..." Groan. "Is going to be harder..." Huff. "Than expected."

He straightened and rested the head of the ax on the ground as he took a break, his breathing raspy and labored.

"That feels good." He closed his eyes, his chest working hard. Some color had come to his face, and he lifted it as if to catch a cool breeze. It gave me a view of the white t-shirt he wore under the blue plaid, and the hormones coursing through my blood highlighted how that spot right there would probably smell as good as his jacket, but more intense. I ground my teeth. As soon as I made it back home, I'd set up a timer and meditate for twenty minutes on the many disadvantages of indulging in an infatuation.

"Wanna try it out?" His eyes sparkled, likely due to the exertion. "It'll come down in a couple of hits."

I shook my head. "No way, thanks. I'm ready to go back home."

"Fine." He swung the ax again. "I can use the release."

I could, too, after his grunting and hard breathing. Meditation would have to do.

He warned me about the tree falling. I helped him wrap it in netting for safe transportation, and we huffed in unison while pulling it on the trolley to the truck, before maneuvering it to the bed. He secured it in place with ropes and expert knots. By the time we were done, I was breathless, too.

"You planned to do all of this by yourself?" I panted.

We stood close; he turned to me. He took off the working gloves, put on his jacket, and stared me down.

I lifted an eyebrow. He put a warm forefinger under my chin and aligned my face with his.

He smirked. "Brawny enough for you?"

I swatted his hand away and he laughed. Damn cocky grump.

My weakness.

When I got home, I meditated for a full half hour.

December 1st

Daniel

NIGHT CLOAKED LAGUNA ISLAND on a cold evening, yet a few hundred people congregated in the main town square. Everyone packed close to each other to keep warm, surrounding the main attraction: the lighting of the tree.

I avoided the masses and strode down the street, the tree to one side and the community hall to the other. The event didn't matter to me, but I had to attend as the co-chair. I had to be there in case of emergencies, and for the meeting afterwards. Hence why I was in search of my co-chair.

It had nothing to do with the pesky little spark in me that threatened to light up into a proper little flame. I wasn't worried about that at all. It would go away. If I remembered correctly from some quick research I had done, the learning mechanism I was looking for was called habituation.

Decreasing my response by repeated presentation to the stimulus.

I found Ale standing behind the still-dark tree, chatting with María, one of the other Christmas Committee members. They both nodded in hello as I joined them.

"I can't promise anything," María said, still in conversation with Ale. "My dad is the right age to be Santa; he is the right size... but he doesn't really like to get out of the house."

"Does he like Christmas, though?" Ale asked. "Maybe he'll get out of the house for the spirit of it all."

"Yeah, he does. Not enough to leave the house most of the time. He didn't come tonight, for example."

Conversations among attendees in the square quieted to a murmur. We couldn't see the podium from our location but, according to the schedule, the Mayor must have taken his place at the mic.

"What if we pay your dad a visit?" I whispered to the two of them. "Could we convince him to do it?"

Ale also spoke in a lower volume, just as the Mayor's speech started.

"We'll probably visit a couple of other options," she said, "but your dad could really be the ticket to solve this issue."

María shrugged. "Again, I can't promise anything, but come next week. I'll butter him up for you."

"Thanks, María." Ale rubbed María's arm and the latter went into the community hall, to help prepare for the post-tree event.

"Everything set up inside?" I asked.

"Yep. I checked in earlier. There's a team finishing up the letters display for the drive, and another team making sure there's coffee and tea available for the donors. Hopefully they sponsor all the gifts."

Right on cue, the mayor reminded the attendees about the drive, and encouraged them to become sponsors.

"I can't believe he's still the Mayor," Ale continued to whisper in my direction. "What is this, his third run?"

"Fourth." I put my hands deep in my pockets to keep them warm. "I think he plans to run again."

Everyone applauded at something the Mayor said, inaudible to us with a change in the wind direction.

"Wow. He might get it, too." She turned to me, and I couldn't help but mirror her. "Anyway, we should try to convince María's dad. I think he's our best bet. I'll still call some of the people on the list my sister sent me again— some of them didn't answer the first time— and see if we can go visit them, too. Can we go next week sometime?"

Habituation required I said yes. The damn spark inside wanted me to say yes, too. Still, I hesitated.

I wrinkled my nose. "I hate the idea of begging for it."

"Who said we're begging?"

"We're visiting grown ass men to ask them for help. We're going to sit there and pretend we agree Christmas matters, and we're going to have to lean into the holiday spirit bullshit." The crowd cheered and applauded again. I checked my watch. Only a few minutes until the tree lighting. "You can't tell me you love that idea?"

"I thought you know the answer by now. I'm not into Christmas either. All the overblown fakeness— not my thing. Going on the road to find Santa doesn't mean I'm going to beg. I'll make perfectly rational, adult arguments about community building. I thought you got that piece? The community building side of things?"

The spark in my gut turned into a silly little flame, at the sight of the playful smirk on her lips, and the subtle arch to her eyebrow. I wanted to erase that smirk. With my lips.

I frowned. "As long as we don't beg. I don't beg."

A grin blossomed on her face. It punched me in the gut. "Don't tempt me with a good time. I might want to challenge you on that."

My breathing quickened. "Don't flirt with me."

Her energy flipped— her smile faltered. I squinted at her and did my best to remain serious.

"I wasn't flirting," she said.

"You were telling me you wanted to make me beg."

"That's not what I meant." Her wide eyes reflected the streetlights around us, her pupils a dark pool. "I meant it would be fun to see you hiding all the grump to ask people to pretty please dress in red and wear a white beard. Making you beg them for help... not begging me— for anything."

"Good. I typically prefer to be the one being begged... for things."

She held my gaze but it cost her. Her shoulders tensed like steeling herself required effort on her part. I shouldn't be teasing her, especially not when I wanted to make it better with a kiss. My eyes dropped to her mouth.

She bit her lip. "Now who's flirting?"

"Not me."

"Not me, either."

The crowd at the other side of the tree started a countdown. *Ten, nine, eight...*

I pursed my mouth. "We were talking about Santa."

"And how we're going to have to swallow our pride and pretend we have enough of a Christmas spirit to desperately ask for a holiday miracle."

Seven, six, five...

"But I'm not begging." I kept my eyes on her, curling my hands to fists in my pockets not to touch her somehow. To pull back from the sudden want coursing through me. To cut the oxygen feeding the fire smouldering inside.

Four, three...

"I'm not begging, either." She held my gaze with resolute eyes.

"No. You'll make rational arguments, I heard."

Two...

"And there will be no flirting, no begging, nothing." Her tone was definite.

"None of it. Neither of us meant it."

One!

The tree lit up all at once. Multicolored strings of light sparkled among the branches; fake snow clustered in a random pattern. Metallic round ornaments hung all around, as did the handmade decorations the town's school children made each year.

Ale and I stared up in unison. My eyes took it all in, ending on the big star at the top. People in the square cheered and applauded.

"Can't deny it's pretty, at least," Ale said at my side.

I gazed at her. The glow from the tree shone on her, highlighting her beauty. Awe glimmered in her eyes. Joy had made its way into the curve of her lips again. No matter what else I felt about her, I couldn't deny she was gorgeous.

That was as much as I could admit to myself. All the rest had to run its course, until the fire burnt every flammable cell in my body, and I felt nothing anymore.

Habituation. That would happen naturally. I could trust habituation.

All the Christmas nonsense would help me get there.

"Pretty?" Tension thinned my lips. "That proves that, out of the two of us, you have the best disposition to… ask for help. At least you like Christmas a little."

"I do not."

"Then explain the look on your face?"

"Shut up. It's an aesthetic appreciation. It's the lights. It's not the season."

"Glad to hear that. I'm going to need some help to survive the holiday."

"We can always laugh about it together, right?"

I nodded and we went inside for the next portion of the evening. If I could laugh about it all, at least it would be a bit easier.

Too bad everyone thought I was a grump.

⸻

Ale

Daniel and I entered the community hall together. I pretended we hadn't spent the past fifteen minutes playing a game of anti-romance whack-a-mole, where both of us did our best to knock our flirting down as hard as we could with verbal mallets. Unfortunately, we hadn't been altogether successful and I didn't know what to make of it.

Without speaking, he went to check on the hot drinks team while I did the same with the group organizing the letters.

"How does the tree look this year?" Janet asked.

"Pretty." I took off my scarf, jacket, and hoodie combo, and hung them all from the back of a chair. I rearranged my sweater around my form, checking that the V-neck showed a bit of the goods, but not too much. "Want to go look? I can keep an eye on things until you're back."

"Thanks!" She put on her puffy jacket and smiled. "My kids are out there with the husband. I'll check on them for a minute and come back ASAP."

"No worries. Enjoy."

She left me and María by the letter wall; this year, we'd made a big sign for the sponsorship drive, and hung the letters from garlands we'd attached to the largest side of the building. The words *Be A Family's Miracle* headlined the night, painted in bright red on light green paper, with gold accents.

Just as Janet made it out of the community hall, people started trickling in from the outside gathering.

"It's all ready," María said. "Perfect."

We moved to the side of the letters and hovered for a while, ready to help if anyone needed. We held on to clipboards and, once someone chose a letter, they came to us so we could write down their names and facilitate the gift donation to families in financial stress.

Forty minutes into the event, Daniel brought María and I coffee.

"How are things going here?" He asked.

"Going well. This is the easiest part. Just waiting around for donors." I sipped from my drink.

"How's the coffee?" He asked us.

"Mine is perfect, thanks." María wrapped her hands around the cup, the clipboard held between her arm and torso.

"This isn't how I drink it, but it's still good."

"How do you drink it?" He asked.

"Doesn't matter." I waved his question away. "It's good. Thanks."

"Hey." An attractive man approached us, a big smile on his face. He showed us the letter he held in his hand, his eyes glued to me. "Can I give you my number?"

Something in his tone told me he had meant more than one thing with the question.

I laughed. "We'll take your number, your email address, and even your name."

I held my clipboard in front of me, pen to paper, and stared at him. I grinned.

"I'm Will." He dictated the rest of his contact information. "Under which circumstances could I expect a call from you?"

I arched an eyebrow. "Once we coordinate with your sponsored family, we'll call you to arrange delivery details."

María hid her humor at Will's flirting behind her coffee cup. To my other side, Daniel glared.

At least this game of whack-a-mole was fun to play. With Will, I didn't have to spend any more time testing boundaries. With him, it was easy to stay off the market— he was attractive, but there was no spark.

"And what about something more casual?" Will asked, no shyness at all. "I don't remember seeing you around. You must have arrived recently, right? I would remember you if I had had the pleasure before."

"That's not going to be possible." Daniel's eyebrows were doing double duty with the way they furrowed. "As the co-chair of the committee, she can't use donors' information that way."

"Shush," I said to Daniel, and turned again to Will. "I appreciate that, but I'm not available."

"Oh, well." Will continued chatting with me, ignoring both María and Daniel. "If you plan to stay in Laguna Island, I'll be around."

"I'll stay, but I can't make any promises."

"Pity. Have a lovely night, everyone." With a final smile, Will left us.

"Does that happen a lot?" María asked. "I don't take it personally; he knows I'm married. But also— wow. He just asked you out, the first time he met you, in front of other people. I didn't know he had that kind of confidence in him. He's typically a quiet guy."

"You never know what quiet guys hide underneath." Daniel grabbed my clipboard and stared at it.

"Or what cranky guys do." I gave Daniel a friendly punch.

He pressed his lips into a thin line, but humor showed in his eyes. "Stop it. I don't have anything to hide."

He gave me back the clipboard.

"Suuuuure."

Mocking him was the perfect plan. What guy liked being made fun of? Anything that had come to life between us could die a slow death that way. Best way to friendzone was to tease their ego. Laughing things off with him would make it less serious, and I needed less serious with him. Then I could just hang out with him for meetings, forget about the tension between us, do my job, and go.

A nice enough time, disguising attraction in camaraderie, until we could go our own ways. If we could make fun of Christmas together, that would be the cherry on top.

December 8

Daniel

A WEEK AFTER THE lighting of the tree, I entered the community hall at my usual cruising speed and made my way to the table where the leading volunteers gathered. Pri, María, Janet, and Hana sat and worked on their tasks, while the larger group of volunteers sprawled over the floor.

I was running a few minutes late but pretended I arrived right on time. The meeting today would include a larger group of people, as we needed the extra hands to work on decorations for the party and gift wrapping for the donation drive. Paper, ribbons, and several types of tape littered every single surface I could see; I ignored it all and grabbed the first chair I found. I took it to the main table and sat down, my to-do list in hand.

Ale was nowhere to be found. Maybe someone had told her of the surprise plan for today, and she'd try to find an excuse not to show up. Or, like me, she'd delayed it as much as she could.

I had suspected she might not want to come to this meeting if she learned of the special plans for it, so I hadn't told her. For the moral support, I preferred it if she were around; it helped to know I could always roll my eyes at her and she'd give me one of those tiny, playful smiles of hers, like I was half-insufferable and half-fun.

The whole thing made her appealing, really— actually, no. Not appealing. Just a kindred spirit. The companionship of it helped; having a co-conspirator in my anti-Christmas sentiment. It was natural that I felt better with her around.

Besides, over the past week we'd moved into a casual friend-ship. She teased me and I took it like a champ. I complained about things, and she gave me a sardonic curl of her lips. It worked.

And that was why, when she entered the hall and strode in the direction of the table, I responded the way I did.

"She needs this chair," I said to Pri by my side.

"What?" Pri held the scissors she'd been using frozen in mid-air, the paper in her other hand flopping slowly.

"Ale's coming this way. She needs this chair."

Janet got up at the other side of the table and went to work with one of the groups on the floor, apparently unaware of the conversation between Pri and I. My neighbor gazed at the empty chair at the other side of the table, then back at me. Technically, Ale could sit where Janet had vacated, but it wouldn't do.

"This chair," I insisted. "Best for Alejandra."

I didn't add anything else. I stared at Pri. Whether I looked antagonistic or sounded nonsensical, it didn't matter to me.

Pri left the scissors on the table, her nostrils flaring, and I gave her a curt nod in thanks. She moved to the other chair and promptly disappeared from my mind, as Ale sat next to me.

"Hey." She gazed around the room. "Well, they're having fun, at least."

Ale, on the other hand, looked like she'd rather be somewhere else.

"Any luck with Santa?" I asked.

"Not really, but there are developments."

She took her phone out of her pocket and gave it to me; she took off her jacket. The movement did something to her sweater, where it tightened around her breasts and belly. The neck of her clothing dropped low enough that it showed me extra skin, and made me think of things I shouldn't be thinking in public.

I couldn't help the way my thoughts of nibbling and licking intensified, when she turned to hang her jacket from the chair. The peek of her bra may have been accidental, but the gorgeous lime color clashed spectacularly, tantalizingly, with her orange and pink hair. If my attention narrowed on it, that was to be expected. Color drew me in, and her skin drew me in. I wanted to fill my hands with flesh, and maybe— maybe — nothing. Looking was supposed to help with habituation but, so far, that plan was going sideways fast.

She didn't seem to notice where my eyes and thoughts had been. She took her cell back and leaned close to me. "Here, look."

She showed me the screen. I forced my eyes away from her and onto her phone.

"I called everyone on the list my sister sent me." She scrolled down the screen; multiple names showed on a spreadsheet in different colors. "Most of them are unavailable for some reason—" she got closer to my ear— "one of them is even dead, but I haven't told Renata yet."

I snorted. She smirked and pulled away.

"There are four likely candidates, but they all want to be courted. Old men, I swear."

I checked my watch. Ten minutes until the surprise. She'd hate it, and so would I.

"Okay. So we're visiting these four candidates, plus María's dad."

"No, four total including María's dad." Ale put her phone away. "I talked to all of them. Next Tuesday afternoon we're going on a rural tour in search of our Santa."

"You said they want to be courted?"

She arched an eyebrow in my direction. "Doesn't mean they're going to get it. Rational arguments, remember?"

"So not begging on your part. What are you willing to do to get what you want out of these old men?"

"Ew, don't say it that way. Why don't you tell me what you're willing to do to get us a Santa?"

I leaned back and crossed my arms. "I'll be your chauffer for an afternoon. That's plenty."

"Pfft." The corner of her lips curled up. "You'll need to do more."

"I refuse to dress in red. You won't catch me wearing the white beard."

"Relax, grumpypants. You won't have to. But you might have to relax that frown and hold back on the eye rolling. You think you can do that? For a few hours?"

"It'll cost me." I gave her the most exasperated look I could muster. "It builds over time if I don't let it out."

She laughed. "You're terrible. What a terrible excuse."

The sound of her laughter pulled a small smile from me. "It's not an excuse. It makes me grind my teeth and my dentist gets mad."

Pri studied us; I ignored her. Ale laughed some more, so I continued.

"The tension builds until I get headaches. And what if my cortisol levels cause permanent cardiac issues?"

"Shut up." Mirth still poured out of Ale. "Cortisol levels, my ass."

Her ass was a risk factor to my cortisol levels, but it might surprise her why. I kept that to myself.

"You should try it out," I said. "Express your irritation when it happens. Don't hold back."

"You're the first person ever to tell me that."

"Doesn't mean I'm wrong."

"You won't make me cranky, Daniel."

The door to the community hall opened, and a string of people of many ages moved in.

"Are you sure about that?" I asked.

The schoolteacher I had talked to a couple days before organized the group into rows. The volunteers in the room quieted down and paid attention; some of them connected the dots and clapped in excitement.

"Oh, no." Ale groaned.

I snorted.

"You win," she said. "This is a nightmare."

The teacher stood in front of the group. She lifted a hand, gave the group a couple of signals, and soon caroling filled the room.

People around us cheered. Applause exploded, then quieted as people returned to work. Except they all joined and started singing, too.

Ale leaned forward on the table, an elbow on the plastic surface. She hid her face with her hand, blocking the view for most people, but I could see her clearly.

Kill me now, she mouthed to me. *I* hate *caroling.*

I laughed. It broke the harmony of the singing, and people around us did a double take at the sound. I didn't care. I simply took the scissors that lay close to Ale and moved them far from her.

I arched an eyebrow. *Just in case.*

She snorted. Then she giggled. I had to purse my lips not to laugh again, which made her laugh.

I'd tried to make her cranky, but I'd ended up having fun with her instead. I chuckled and shook my head.

I stood and pulled her up from her arm. "Come. Let's go get warm drinks for everyone."

She didn't fight me. We put our jackets back on and I guided her to rEvalution, Eva's coffee shop at the other side of the square.

"I texted her this morning to have the order ready right around now," I said as we walked across the plaza.

We strolled past the big center fountain, the trees and gazebo, and flower beds. The town may not have been in the best financial situation, but the square had been maintained well. It was a spot where the town showed its pride.

"So you knew about the caroling?" Ale elbowed me.

"I can't confirm or deny."

"You so knew! That's just evil."

"I also found a way to rescue us from it, didn't I?"

"Sure, I'll give you that."

I opened the door for Ale at rEvalution. The smell of coffee welcomed us like a hug. Several tables and chairs, and a couple of sofas occupied the front room by the big windows. By one of the side walls, big built-ins held books for people to borrow, magazines and newspapers, and even a basket with multiple types of device chargers. A huge painting of Laguna Island hung on the back wall; it portrayed the bay, with its tiny island and old mansion tucked to the side, and a hint of the small lake at the top of it that gave the town its name. To the other side wall sat the counter behind which Eva conducted business, and the food displays all around in a big L. The options included Latin American sweet and savory pastries, cakes, empanadas, and sopaipillas. The door to the back space was dark behind her.

Eva glanced at us with her usual business-like stare. "I have your order ready. There's enough eggnog in that coffee to make a few folks tipsy. And the peppermint crystals I added to the cookies will make them go wild."

"Thanks, Eva." I paid her for everything while she brought the two big coffee dispensers and boxes of sweets from the back. "I'm going to guess you don't like eggnog," I said to Ale. "Can I get you something you'll like? It will help us cope with all that cheer in the hall."

"Yes, thanks. I'll have coffee with a splash of cream. No sugar. Thanks, Eva."

Eva put the food in one big bag for easy carrying and grabbed a tray for Ale's and my drinks. With incredible efficiency, she moved onto the POS screen to set up our orders.

I paid again. "I'll have it black, like my soul during the holidays."

Ale snorted. "Why is it so hard to escape all the Christmas nonsense, do you think? It's not that it was easy in the City, but it's even worse here."

Eva was the one to respond, her hands moving fast over her industrial espresso machine. "It's because we see all the same faces every day, and they're all smiling at us and fully expecting a smile in return. We don't get to stroll among anonymous people power-walking to their destinations. Everyone wants to stop and ask how you're doing, and don't you love the season?"

I nodded in agreement. I stopped often to get good quality coffee and snacks from Eva, and she was one of the few people I thought of as a friend in town. We had similar personalities; she also was no-nonsense and focused intently on bringing life back to Laguna Island. On a couple of occasions, I'd even kept her company while she closed up shop, and we'd dreamed about how to fix the town to make it the paradise we knew it could be.

"Eva!" Ale said. "I didn't know you also have something against the holidays."

My friend pushed our cups to us and shrugged. "I'm indifferent to them, but I do get annoyed at how over the top it gets."

"Can I count on no Christmas music from your speakers, then?" Ale tasted her drink. "Wow. This is amazing."

"I play Christmas songs the last few days before the twenty-fifth. That's it."

I smiled. "We should form a club. We won't survive it in the future, otherwise. At least Renata will be doing well next year and I won't have to be on the committee."

"Are you going to preside over the committee next year, too, Daniel?" Eva asked.

"Never again. I'll figure out a way to get out of it moving forward. There will be other ways to promote community bonding."

"Like buying all this coffee for people." Eva raised an eyebrow. "Making them happy and helping the local business, right?"

"Oh, no. This is selfish." My mouth tilted with humor. I grabbed one of the coffee dispensers and the bag with food; Ale would take the other dispenser and our drinks. "If they're drinking warm drinks and stuffing their mouths with cookies, they can't sing carols."

"No, I think Eva and I know your secret," Ale said. "You're less cranky than people think. You're actually sharing in the cheer with this."

"Please. That doesn't sound like me, does it?"

"It does," Eva said with a restrained smile.

I frowned. "In that case, you two should know you're crankier than people know. I'm not afraid to use that information to my advantage."

"I'm not that bad," both Ale and Eva said.

"Me neither, you hear me? Better if we all keep these revelations private."

December 12

DANIEL HADN'T STOPPED FROWNING for the past two hours. It was a wonder the muscles of his brow weren't shaking with the effort. Then again, if he kept this gesture on his face a lot, then maybe they were strong enough to sustain the frown for hours. Like he had.

"Thank you for having us in your home," I told María. We'd spent the past half hour visiting, trying to convince her dad to be our Santa. The three of us stood by her door saying goodbye. "Do you think he'll do it?"

"I don't know." She stole a glance at Daniel and brought it right back to me. "He didn't seem very happy at the idea. I've been trying to get him excited about it, but... cranky people can be a tough nut to crack."

She cast her eyes at Daniel, who squinted back.

"Don't worry. I can work with cranky people." I winked at María and Daniel snorted next to me. "Would you talk to your dad some more? He's our best option."

María nodded. "I'll keep trying. Beneath the grouchy exterior, he actually likes children."

"Well, thank you. I'll text you, okay?"

We said goodbye; Daniel practically ran down the porch steps. I thought he'd sprint to the pickup truck, but he offered me his hand to come down the stairs, like I didn't have a rail. I took it and ignored the comforting warmth of it; I let go as soon as I stepped on solid, wet ground again.

We got back in the truck, Daniel at the wheel as he'd been all afternoon.

"You're done, aren't you?" I asked.

"So done." He drove us down the rough gravel path leading away from the farm. "We've been to four houses in five hours. It's getting dark, it smells like rain's coming, and we still have no Santa."

"I think Manuel— the second one— he might do it if we can't get María's dad to agree. Otherwise... you might have to do it."

"The fuck I am. What about you, Ms. President?"

"Mr. President, I don't have the voice for it. Listen to this— ho, ho, ho."

It sounded pitiful. He snorted, then laughed. His frown relaxed.

He shook his head. "I'm not the president. I'm the liaison for the local government."

"Then... am I the boss?"

The road was rough in this rural section; trees spotted the land around us, breaking the farmland landscape of rolling hills, crops, and animals.

"No," Daniel replied. "You're the president of the volunteers, but we co-chair. We're equals."

"I can be the boss if you prefer it. Only then I'd consider wearing the Santa costume."

The skies opened with no warning. Rain fell fast and heavy on the windshield. The evening darkened swiftly; Daniel turned on the headlights.

"Fuck. The lights are dim," he said.

"That sounds bad."

"It means the battery is probably dying. Shit. I hope we don't get stuck."

"As long as we make it back home, we'll be fine. Let's be optimistic."

"I know we haven't known each other for long, but what part of this—" he waved a hand in front of his face— "depicts optimism?"

Rain obscured the windshield. Daniel upped the speed of the wipers.

I laughed. "Okay, guilty. But you moved here with an optimistic plan, and I'm pretty confident saying that."

"And see how well that's going? I knew it would be tough, but I didn't know the town was in this much trouble."

A flutter of worry gripped my stomach at the road ahead of us, both figuratively and literally.

The frown made a return. It was scary to think the town was doing this poorly, but also not surprising. Since its glory days in the 90s, Laguna Island had lost people and resources in equal measure.

"There has to be a way out of this," I said.

"Out of running out of battery? Nothing but crossing our fingers."

"No. Out of this spiral of decline the town is caught in."

"I'm trying, Ale. I really am. But we need to suddenly make everyone richer for extra tax income, get grants, a benefactor, or straight up sell the town."

For a moment, the sound of rain on roof and glass overtook everything else.

"How bad are things? Actually?"

"Bad. After the boom in the 90s, with those waves of recession and people leaving..." he sighed. "Laguna Island has suffered for the past couple of decades. But Eva and I have a plan. I'm targeting the local government, and Eva has the townspeople. I'll write so many money applications at the start of next year that I'm going to wear out the keys on my laptop. We just need a few million dollars to appear from somewhere."

"That's the only thing, huh? No wonder you're grumpy all the time."

He chuckled. "I make no promises. Those millions don't guarantee a great mood for the rest of my life... but it would help. If you hear anything, let me know."

I scoffed. "I wish. If I find a billionaire with a good heart somewhere, I'll let you know."

"Shit." All the stress that had slowly left him returned full force in that single word, as he tightened his grip on the wheel.

"What?!"

"The tire light came on." He slowed down the truck. "What the hell happened? I was worrying about the battery!"

With the vehicle at a full stop now, he pulled his jacket zipper up. "Crap. I'm going to have to keep it idling. I can't risk it with the battery."

He got out of the truck and circled it, checking the tires. The sound of rain was all that kept me company until he returned, his hair completely wet. Drops ran down the fabric of his jacket.

He leaned on the wheel in defeat. "The rear left tire is losing air fast. It has an inch-wide gash."

Night continued to advance, darkness cloaking the open space around us more and more with every passing minute.

I stared down the road, dread cooling me down. "How far are we from town?"

"Let's not worry about that first. The spare tire should help. I hope."

His tone didn't exude a lot of trust in the spare tire.

He got out of the truck again. Restlessness took over me fast; I didn't like being left alone in the truck. I distracted myself by texting my sister.

> **Ale**: I'm going to be late. Everything's fine, just a little hiccup on the road.

> **Ren**: Are you okay? Should I call someone? What's going on?

> **Ale**: Just a problem with a tire. I'm with Daniel. Everything's going to be okay. I just didn't want you to worry that I'm late.

> **Ren**: ok. Let me know if you're running out of phone battery or something and update me as you can

> **Ale**: for sure <3

Daniel returned and I breathed a sigh of relief.

"I'm sorry, Ale. I'm going to need your help. It's getting dark fast. If you can hold the flashlight, I can move faster."

"Of course!"

"We have an umbrella somewhere but there's no point in using it. The wind is too intense. And we'll have to get on the ground. It'll make you wet and dirty. I'm sorry."

"I don't mind. Wet and dirty can be fun." I winked; he smirked and shook his head. I put up my hood and hid as many strands into it as I could. "Show me what I need to do."

He focused first on unscrewing the nuts and pulling the torn tire off, while I held the flashlight. He'd been right; the wind made everything worse. Rain quickly dampened my clothes, and soon the air currents had pulled the hood off my hair.

Daniel threw the old tire into the truck bed and rummaged for cardboard. He only found a small piece. We moved to the back of the vehicle; the spare tire was affixed under the bed. He placed the cardboard on the ground for me, so I could kneel and point the flashlight in the right direction. Daniel full-on lay on the ground and, wrench in hand, he slid in the mud to work on the spare tire. From the sounds and expletives that reached me occasionally, he worked as hard as he could. I soon stopped bothering to clean my glasses from rain drops.

Cold water dripped down my back, finding the small space between my skin and my clothes. I helped him get the spare tire out and get off the ground just as I started to shiver.

"Just a bit longer," he said.

But the rain and wind had chilled my bones by the time the spare tire was in place and we were able to hide in the cab again.

"Take off your jacket." He unzipped his jacket and unbuttoned his shirt. "Your sweater too, if it's wet. Water is going to keep you too cold."

He undressed to his undershirt; I peeled off the outer layers of clothing. He threw his coat and flannel to the back seat and came back forward with a blanket. I threw my jacket and sweater back, to join his muddy clothes.

Shivers ran through me. My nipples hurt, the cold had made them pebble so hard... and his eyes seemed to notice it.

He tore his eyes away from my chest and upped the heated air. "We need to get going soon, if we don't want to worry about gas as well. Here, take it."

He handed me the blanket.

I pursed my lips. My next move had to be decided in a split second. It was probably a bad idea, but I leaned toward him. The center console between us, I wrapped the blanket around both of us.

"It's okay," he said. "The blanket isn't big enough."

"Come on, get cozy. We can make it work. Let's warm up for five minutes. The battery will be fine."

He hesitated. I held the corners of the blanket tight in my hand, keeping it around us. Shoulder to shoulder, we shared in warmth.

His eyes dropped to my lips, then came back up full of intensity. Yep, a bad idea to cozy up to him, but I didn't regret it. I couldn't let him get a cold because being close to him made me nervous. Because based on the way he looked at me, he was attracted to me, too.

His hand lifted between us. My skin warmed up in anticipation to his touch; his fingers hovered by the curve of my jaw. My lips tingled, because he might kiss me... and I would let him. He got closer, but his hand didn't rest on my face.

With slow passes of his fingers, he wiped the water from my glasses. He smiled, friendly, except for the challenging arch of his eyebrow.

I had wanted him to kiss me. I wasn't supposed to want it. Not from him, nor anyone. But my stomach still ached with want.

"You're welcome." His voice rumbled low, a tease hidden in the simple words.

I rolled my eyes. Better not to think of how close I'd been to letting my weakness break me.

"Thanks." I bit my lip and leaned on the center console. It would be best if I kept it friendly and casual, and aimed for small talk. "So, tell me. Why did you move to Laguna Island? You said you thought it was doing better than it is?"

We remained shoulder-to-shoulder but, while he still gazed at me, I focused on the dark road ahead of us; the sight was blurry, thanks to streaks of dirt and dried drops I hadn't bothered to clean from my glasses. Rain continued to batter the roof, but at least warmth seeped into my skin.

With no warning or hesitation, Daniel gently removed the glasses from my face and I let him, curious to see what he'd do with them.

He wiped them with the corner of the blanket. "No. I knew it was struggling, just not this badly. But I didn't want the picket fence and 2.5 kids in the suburbs. I don't want that married, city life. I came here to have the life I want. A few good friends, a community, and a cozy apartment to hide in and read for an evening. Reconnecting with some of my Latine roots, since the town has that vibe thanks to all the immigrants that made a home here. It's still the plan in the long term."

"I see."

He checked the glasses were clean again and carefully put them back on. "Why did you ask?"

He seemed to concentrate on his task, with oh so much non-chalance. Like we did this every day. Like he looked into my eyes that way all the time.

I took a slow, deep breath. "To be friendly. Get to know you a bit more. "

"And?"

And my attempt at small talk had failed. I didn't feel friendlier towards him, but the want continued to build right under my skin.

I couldn't give him that answer, so I shared a different truth.

"I think I understand you better. You're not typically as grumpy as the town thinks you are. You like your solitude. You're willing to work hard to get what you want. Makes me like you."

Which was the whole problem.

The corner of his lips lifted a smidge. "I think I get you, too. You came back because you love your sister, but you love the town, too. You take things in stride. Few things actually ruin your mood, one of which is Christmas. You're good with grumps. Makes me like you, too."

His eyes dropped to my lips again.

Okay, then. Time to put down some boundaries.

"I am not in the market," I said.

His eyes came back to mine. "And I don't want a settled suburban life."

The rain continued to fall around us, still relentless.

"I didn't say that was the problem." My eyes didn't waver on his. "I don't want that either."

"Then what's the problem?"

"I don't want anything for a while."

"I don't think I want anything, ever."

"Then we're good. Maybe we'll end up friends."

"Maybe we will. We're good."

He gave me a reticent smile and let me have the blanket while he drove me back home.

December 15

Daniel

THE GAZEBO IN THE town square had been covered in red and green garlands, in preparation for the cookie decoration competition. About a hundred people surrounded it; they faced the platform and the table set up in it, where the contest would take place.

Ale stood alone by the table, and the sight of her interrupted the signals keeping my lungs working at a constant rhythm. That was the likely reason for the way my breath hitched. All because of the way she dressed.

I hadn't braced myself to see Ale in an elf costume.

I frowned and strode to the gazebo with a strange flutter in my gut. Were these the famous butterflies people talked about? If so, this was terrible news. It meant that my attraction to Ale hadn't decreased by spending time with her, rather, it continued to grow.

Maybe science had failed me, but the new evidence explained why I had almost kissed her in the truck a few days before. Habituation was nowhere to be found. My feelings had intensified. Fuck. At least, Ale and I agreed: we would not pursue anything we might be feeling.

A new confidence fueled my steps as I climbed the stairs onto the platform. It encouraged me to admire Ale's body like it wouldn't have much of an impact on me. I gazed at her shapely, full legs in white and red striped tights; her forest-green little dress, with a skirt that somehow both highlighted her thick thighs and her plush ass; and a ridiculous red-green hat combo that clashed with her fun hair. And it made me want to devour her. Oops.

It. Would. Go. Nowhere.

I gulped and approached her. The fact that Ale frowned as intensely as I did distracted me. She seemed half-irritated, half-panicked, by the way her lips pressed tight and her eyes opened wide.

"This is quite the development," I said. "What an outfit."

"Don't start." She glared in my direction. "I was coerced."

"By whom? Who do I need to scare off with a harsh look and stern words? How dare they do this to you."

Six trays of cookies lay covered on the table, with no other markings. That way, the competition would be anonymous and impartial.

"My sister and Janet. Don't be mean to my sister though."

"It wouldn't be fair to be mean to Janet alone."

She sighed. "Then don't be mean to her, either. She was the one who was going to wear this costume and judge the cookie decoration competition. She can't now because her whole family came down with a cold."

"This can't be Janet's costume?" I gazed down her body again. Couldn't help myself. "This looks too good on you to be meant for someone else."

Feelings may have intensified, and I may have been counting on them going away eventually, but it didn't mean I had to lie. She looked *hot*. Casual flirting was harmless; casual friends could flirt. Right? Because it wouldn't lead anywhere.

She cut me a glance. "No. It's my sister's."

"She just had a sexy elf dress in her closet?"

"Yes. She wears it every year. She probably wore it last year too."

The vague memory of Renata in an elf costume came back to me from the previous Christmas. I didn't remember it catching my eye the way it did when wrapping Ale's body.

When it wrapped Ale's body, it made me want to grab her by the waist and pull her to me.

By the way she squinted at me, I had broadcast the intention for anyone to see.

I cringed. This went beyond casual flirting. It crossed a line. This was about *her* and what I wanted to do to *her*.

"Anyway." A brief escape was my best option. "Good luck judging. I'll come back when the competition starts."

She seemed happy to follow my lead on that.

"I'm sure you can't wait to witness my pain."

"Yeah. You hide your hatred for Christmas well. No one else seems to see it, but someone has to."

"You just really want someone to share in your misery."

I winked and walked away.

"Ugh, I hate sweets," she said.

I chuckled and left without looking back.

For the next twenty minutes, I focused on making sure things were going right throughout the town square. Except that I couldn't stop stealing glances at the gazebo. Ale looked like she prepared to offer herself as a sacrificial lamb.

I didn't need to do something about it... it was a bad idea to devise a plan to rescue her... but I truly wanted to. I wanted to so hard, that it showed me just how into Ale I was.

The whole thing should have convinced me to retreat. I repeated it to myself every time I talked to someone to help me out with my plan. But I was terrible at depriving myself and went through with it anyway.

By the time I came back to the covered platform, I carried a to-go cup and two people followed me.

"Okay." I gave Ale a rEvalution cup of coffee I'd bought for her. "Some cream, no sugar. Should help you survive the next hour."

She grabbed the cup, face blank except for wide-open eyes. Like she didn't know how to react.

I smirked. "I brought extra judges. This is Sebastián, who's an expert because he's a six-year-old kid. This is his mom, Leslie, who is an expert because she makes a big selection of the cookies Eva sells at rEvalution. You're the third judge, who can come in to decide the vote if needed, on criteria such as decoration, for example." I leaned in and whispered into her ear. "Best I could do on short notice. You're welcome."

A smile blossomed on her face. "Thank you, Daniel."

Her eyes stayed on me and, yes. I was pretty sure now my stomach was full of butterflies.

"Where's Santa?" Sebastián asked.

Ale bent down, one hand holding her coffee and the other on her knee, looking adorable. "He was busy in another town, so he sent me to help him out."

Leslie stared at me with a weird look.

"What are you looking at?" I asked her.

She pulled her lips to the side and shook her head.

"You look like Renata," the kid insisted in Ale's direction.

"It's because I'm her Elf twin," she said. "She sent me a letter to the North Pole and told me about Santa not being available, so I came to help."

Sebastian's eyes grew ten sizes. "Do I have an Elf twin?"

"Yes! We all do. You just need to be older to meet them."

"Why?"

"Uhm… Christmas… magic?" She gave me a panicked look and I smirked. "Well. When is the competition starting?"

I checked my watch. We were on time. "You call the competitors up. I'll organize them."

Coffee still in hand, she grabbed the mic from the table and started the show.

"Cookie Cooks, come up one by one!"

The crowd cheered as the competitors approached the gazebo; Ale asked for their name and invited them to line up next to the table. I uncovered the cookies and guided them all on where exactly to stand.

Ale introduced Leslie and Sebastián as the judges.

"Are you judging, too?" One of the participants asked me.

I shook my head. "Nope. It would ruin the system."

Not to say anything about ruining my appetite with so much sugar.

"You could replace me." Ale asked as she approached.

"Why would I want to do that?" I whispered as Leslie and Sebastián began stuffing their bodies with Christmas cookies. "Besides, you just announced you'd be the third judge."

"Fine. Will you be the MC then?"

I rolled my eyes like it cost me to be the MC, but took the mic from her.

I spoke in a monotonous voice. "Cheer and joy. Cookies are great. Once we have a winner, you'll get one to share."

I did nothing to put excitement into it. In fact, I was certain the words dripped with boredom and antagonism. I got a few side eyes from the participants, but Ale laughed.

"You're terrible. Give that to me." She took the mic again and went on to interview the participants, while Leslie and Sebastián continued to taste the cookies. For the next several minutes, the contestants told us about their favorite seasonal memories.

I limited myself to hovering with arms crossed and, a little while later, holding Ale's coffee for her. It still warmed my hand when Leslie and Sebastián approached us to discuss the winner. We moved to the back of the gazebo for privacy as we heard their opinion.

"Totally," Ale said. "I'm on board. Sounds like a unanimous decision!"

I snorted; she'd managed to not taste a single cookie and kept the whole competition moving along. Just my kind of people, but she did it with a smile.

"Let's give them their prize." I nodded at her.

Ale asked the participants to stand behind their cookies; I joined her at the front of the platform, with Leslie and Sebastián.

"Will you do the honors, little person? Stand in front of the winning cookies." Ale gave Sebastián a gentle push, and he jumped to stand in front of one of them.

"Carol wins this year's cookie competition!" Ale exclaimed.

Attendants clapped and cheered; Carol smiled and applauded in excitement. Ale asked Leslie to talk about what made Carol the winner; the latter talked about balance of spices and flavor, plus great decoration, while I grabbed the prize: a framed painting of mistletoe by the school kids, with a drawn banner reading, WINNER.

Carol displayed the award to everyone on the square; they continued to clap as the other participants began distributing the cookies among the crowd.

I turned the mic off. With everyone sharing in the cookies, the event would end soon.

"Why mistletoe?" Ale got her coffee back and sipped from it.

She and I stood to the side of the platform, where the stairs and main pillars met. Leslie and Sebastián chatted with Carol next to us, while everyone else mingled and enjoyed their sweets.

"Who knows," I replied. "The kids come up with this stuff. Mistletoe is a pest. And people think it's romantic? As if."

She chuckled. "I thought the tradition with mistletoe is about... erm... fecundity."

"You're not wrong. It can multiply fast and it's parasitic. And yet you have an old-time guy, thinking it would be cute to bring mistletoe from Europe for the sake of the season, so he brings it from over and makes a fuuuuu—" I stole a glance at Sebastián, who paid attention to our conversation. "A *fun* farm of it and it really makes no sense. It spread all over, sometimes overtaking the natural North American type—"

"You're standing under the mistletoe." Sebastián pointed a straight finger above our heads.

Ale and I stared up at the offending branch in unison. A dark green twig with white berries and a red ribbon hung above us.

We stared at each other for a moment. I waited to see what she would do. When she said nothing, I did the heroic thing and gave her an out.

"We don't have to do this."

"We just established the mistletoe thing is ridiculous."

And dangerous, in my opinion. One thing was to struggle with butterflies and feelings, another with what could happen after I kissed her.

"You have to!" Sebastián insisted. "Dad says it's important to keep traditions."

"Come on, it's just a bit of fun!" Leslie caught on to her son's excitement and joined in. "It's kind of cute; you're the co-chairs of the town celebrations."

Sebastián practically jumped in his spot with excitement. Leslie smiled at us like she had a little secret. I frowned.

Carol joined them. "Do it for the kid!"

"For the town!" Someone said from the crowd.

Soon word of what we were up to moved through the crowd.

People in the front, near the platform, started clapping rhythmically. Soon most attendees added to it in *encouragement*.

I released an exasperated sigh. "They'll stop if we just do it."

"Fine. A quick peck." Ale rolled her eyes.

I raised an eyebrow. "If you dread it so much, we don't have to do it. They can be disappointed; it won't kill them."

"I don't dread it, I just…"

"It's just a peck." I took her chin with two fingers, brought her face to me, and dropped a kiss on her mouth.

Her lips were soft— I didn't get to register much more. The surprise made her pull back; I immediately let her go and did my best to kill the damn flying insects taking over my gut. Except Ale took over and kissed *me*, like a second thought had made her want to do it again. More. Properly.

The second touch of our lips turned my insides into a flame. Heat ignited on my skin. It anchored me in my place; it told me I should kiss her a thousand times more. The kiss, short and simple as it was, begged me to do something about what I felt, whether it made sense or not.

For a moment I didn't hear the cheering and clapping around us. It took until Ale pushed me away with a hand on my chest for me to register them. Or the way I had seemed to cling onto her waist in the middle of the kiss.

Sebastián laughed, while the competitors joined everyone in the crowd with a smile. Leslie gave me a funny look as I blinked a few times.

"I did it for the town," I said.

"I'm sure," Leslie winked. She turned to Ale. "You *are* good with grumps."

"Right." Ale said nothing else.

In complete silence, Ale and I put away the table and took it back to the community hall. We didn't speak of the kiss as we made plans to visit our two main Santa contenders again, either.

Just like me, it seemed that Ale planned to ignore the fact something had clicked with that simple peck.

Only that I still didn't see the point in lying, and the evidence of the past few hours made it clear. Waiting for it to pass wouldn't do. So what could I do instead?

December 18

WHEN DANIEL CAME FOR me in the usual pickup truck to visit our two top Santa contenders, I didn't expect to end the night in a tiny bar at the edge of town.

This place had existed ever since I could remember, but I hadn't been there before. The walls in The Silo were dark brown and full of framed photos; a mix of sepia pictures of the area, farm labourers, as well as people I assumed were regulars made up most of the décor. The dim lights gave the space an old-fashioned but cozy feel, like the place was affixed to the rural side of Laguna Island. It probably was.

Daniel and I sat in a booth at the back, hidden from the surrounding farmers and their families. He'd explained this establishment served people living outside of the town limits and had a family-oriented vibe.

"I'm more of an outsider here," he said. "I come when I want to be left the hell alone."

A few glasses littered the space between us. We celebrated the fact that we'd found Santa. María's dad had agreed to it. He grumbled and made it clear the whole deal irritated him, but he'd said yes.

"I understand him," Daniel said. "I'm like him. Grumpy, wanting to be by myself except when I don't, and willing to make sacrifices for the community."

I laughed. "You're not that bad."

"You say that because we click. We're more similar than we're different. Even if you don't show your grump with people."

"I'm not grumpy. There may be some... seasonal irritation showing, but I don't think that's a reason to ruin it for other people."

"I don't know. At first I thought you're the kind of person who gets annoyed easily, but feels bad about being cranky, so you bite your tongue."

I finished my third drink of the night, a delicious Old-Fashioned in honor of the feelings I got when entering the pub. The orangey taste coated my tongue, and I took a deep breath to intensify the taste.

I pushed the glass aside. "I always speak up when it matters. Also, I believe you can always say what you think, it just takes finesse sometimes to say it kindly."

"I think the right people for you will like you even when you say things with a little meanness." He sipped from his drink, a fruity type— I didn't ask what it was, but it surprised me that a rough-around-the-edges guy would drink the sweeter stuff.

"The right people for *you*, that is. Right?" I smirked. "Because from the sounds of it, you need someone who won't care that you're going to be just like María's Dad when you're old."

"Excuse me? I'm like him *now*. Have I not made it clear?"

I pursed my lips to the side, to tamper my instinct to chuckle. I usually laughed a grump's antics off, but the drink was making it worse. "And he has people who like him as he is. I think."

"I do, too. I know people here appreciate how hard I'm working to make things better."

"Because that's how you compensate for it. Hah! That's the final puzzle piece. You're one of those people who are irritable but will mow an elderly person's lawn for free and expect no thanks."

"Yeah. And I'm okay with that." He finished his drink. "No need to wait to get old to act like an old man. I may switch to button down sweaters soon to stress the point."

The image stole another laugh out of me.

"Ready to go home?" He asked, a half-smile tilting his lips.

"How are we going to go home? We've been drinking a lot." I made a show of all the empty glasses on the table.

"I'm driving us." He got up and offered me my hoodie and jacket; he put on his own.

"What?" I put on my outer layers and gave Daniel a hard stare. "No way you can get behind the wheel after all of this. We may have to walk or..."

There were no cabs on Laguna Island.

He dug his hands in his jacket pockets. "Thing is... you know how I insisted to go get our drinks at the bar instead of asking Millie to tend to us?"

"Yeah. You said you wanted to make it easier on her."

"Yep. It was also because that way I could ask Alfredo to make me non-alcoholic drinks. My first glass was the only one that had alcohol in it. I'm good to drive."

He gazed at me with patience, and it settled clearer in me. This was his brand of kindness, allowing me to safely enjoy the evening. It was also my ultimate weakness. A grump that was there for you, no questions asked.

The locks I'd put around my attraction for him opened all at once. I had wanted to be unavailable, but he'd made his way into my feelings anyway, sowing seeds that could grow if I let them.

When I didn't answer right away, he added, "I didn't think you'd relax enough if you didn't think I was drinking, too."

He shrugged. I squirmed, mostly uncomfortable in my realization.

"I assumed we'd walk..." I let out, lost at what else to say for the moment.

"It's a half hour walk in the dark. It's cold. It's fine. I'll drive. Should we go?"

I nodded and followed him out of The Silo. He opened the door for me and, as soon as I stepped outside, the cold air shocked my body.

"Oh shit." My head swam. "I'm drunk now."

He put his arm around me. "Are you really? Didn't seem like it a minute ago."

We stood right outside the bar, lonely in the parking lot, standing on gravel in the night.

"El aire me pegó." I stared at him. "Do you speak Spanish?"

"The air hit you," he translated. He guided me to the truck. "My mom taught me. I understand it better than I speak it. Will you be okay?"

"I think so. Just... Let's see what happens when you start driving."

Luckily, I didn't feel sick. The alcohol did seem to loosen my tongue.

"I mean," I argued, though Daniel wasn't speaking much. We'd been on the road for ten minutes and had another ten or so left. "I know exactly what you did. You asking for non-alco... holic... drinks— it was you mowing my lawn. Wasn't it?"

He snorted. "Sure. Yeah."

"So, Dan. Danny?"

"Let's keep it as Daniel."

"What about Daniel en español." Accordingly, I pronounced his name in a Latin American Spanish accent. "I hate when people read my name and say *ale*. Like the drink. I'm not fermented grains!"

"Only call me Daniel—" he pronounced it the same way I had— "if you want me to think of my mom."

"Okaaay. Ugh, you're cranky. But I like it, somehow? What I don't like is Christmas."

"Why don't you like it, again?"

"It's like the epi— epitome of toxic positivity. I hate toxic positivity."

"Agreed—"

"—you did say we click!—" I interrupted him nonsensically.

"— and the way it's forced consumerism as well." He continued as if I hadn't said anything. "From October to December—"

"The Ber months are supposed to be fun!" I hit my thigh with my palm. "Christmas isn't fun."

"—we're pushed all this themed stuff. But what is *really* special about it? Nothing but the convention of some monthly holidays."

We entered the urban zone of the town, simple one-story houses around us.

"We do click I think," I added.

He cleared his throat. "The things they say make the holidays special are things that should happen all year long. Being good to one another, being grateful..."

"Being witchy!"

"Doing what you can to help people. Joy, though, that's a stretch. Things can be difficult."

"I have a fantasy." I frowned.

We stopped at a red light. The streets were empty, no other cars in sight. But he didn't drive through the crossing.

He stared at me, eyes open wide. Pupils widening. "You have a... fantasy."

"Yeah." I glanced at his lips, then back at his steady eyes. "You know what would be amazing?"

"Mhh?"

The simple syllable sounded strangled for some reason.

"Getting a spray can and writing Christmas Can Suck It on a wall." I cackled.

"Oh." He snorted. "You fantasize about vandalism. Interesting."

That made my laugh turn wilder. "Yes! I will never admit this to anyone, but I do wonder what it would be like to just open my mouth and let things come out as I think them."

"You can actually try, you know." He went back to driving, long past the time the lights had turned green. We approached the main square.

"Maybe. But until I do... I'll fantasize about being mean with spray paint."

He laughed. "That's what you call mean? *Christmas can suck it*?"

"Well... Yeah. It's not mean. But it's my fantasy, okay?"

"Okay." He parked the truck by the square, on a side perpendicular to the lit-up Christmas tree.

"What are we doing?"

"I'm going to make your dreams come true."

I stilled. "Wait. What? How—"

"Come on. You're half-way drunk. Aire no pega again, right? This will be fun."

I smiled at his cute, slightly incorrect Spanish. He grinned back, and the locks that had opened earlier fell right to the floor.

He got out of the truck and rummaged in the back; I got out and followed unsteadily.

"What are you doing?" I stood next to him.

The truck bed had a metal box with tools, and Daniel rummaged in it. "Ah-ha! I knew I had one in the truck. Do you see this?"

He held a spray can up to me.

"We're not actually doing it, are we?" I crossed my arms, a little bit because of the cold, and a lot so I wouldn't reach for the can.

"Yes, we are." He grabbed me by my arm and pulled.

I resisted a bit; his hand slid down my forearm until he held my hand. He linked our fingers like it was nothing, no big deal. And pulled some more. I had no choice but to follow him again.

How far would he take me, if I let him?

He stopped at a crossroads, leaving us smack in the middle. The streets remained empty; we were alone. Only the streetlights and stop signs kept watch.

We stood next to each other with interlocked fingers.

The corner of Daniel's lips curled up. "Listen. We're going to do it. This is your fantasy, isn't it?"

"It is, but— when people see it tomorrow..."

"It's going to be fine. This is chalk paint. It'll go away with the first rain. Considering where we live, it won't last more than a few hours. A day at most."

"Oh." Relief rushed through me. "That's different."

"So? Are we doing it?" He offered the can, shaking it in front of me.

His lips stretched into a smile. I grabbed the can and giggled. Damn alcohol.

Still holding his hand, I wrote *Xmas Sux* in big letters on the pavement.

He laughed. "Yes! Good girl. Or should I say, bad girl?"

"Call me a good girl all you want."

"I like it when you're feisty."

He took the can from me and added an angry face next to the words. "There. Now I'm not just an accessory to the crime. I have blood on my hands."

Daniel offered the can back, but I shook my head. He put it in one of his pockets and hooked his thumb from it.

We still held hands; turning to face each other happened naturally. Being accomplices brought us closer, to a place where we could just exist. Him with his sharp disposition, me not caring. Me rolling my eyes at him, and him liking it.

"The town still doesn't have surveillance cameras, right?" I gazed up at him. "There's no recording of us doing this, I hope?"

"Nothing. No one will know but you and me." His voice deepened.

I resisted it. "It'll be the talk of the town tomorrow." I took a picture with my phone and put it right back in my pocket. "There. I'll always remember. Thank you."

"You're welcome." He stepped closer to me.

"I appreciate you doing this for me. And everything else. For someone who's irritable and always talks about wanting to be alone, you're quite kind with your fellow townspeople."

He got closer. I gulped.

He took my other hand in his. "I'm not kind with everyone. But it seems I'm kind with you."

"Why is that?" The words came out soft, barely held in the breath that left me at his proximity.

"I like being alone, you're right." He angled his head toward me. I couldn't help but align mine to his lips. "But I think I also like being alone... with you."

"It hasn't even been a week since we said we wouldn't do anything about this."

"I know."

And I don't care.

I heard the words clearly in my mind, but I didn't know if they were uttered in his voice or mine.

The touch of his lips flipped a switch in my muscle memory. Sensations burst and travelled through my body, reminding me of the kiss under the mistletoe, and how much more I had wanted at the time. He pressed his mouth to mine and it came right back, that want. It roared inside, a sudden rumble behind by breastbone, asking what else he could do; what more would I feel if I kissed him back.

I did. I opened my lips and glued myself to him, arms around his shoulders. His curls were silk against my fingers, as I dug into his hair. His tongue explored my mouth and he surrounded me with his arms. He pulled me close, and I went to the tip of my toes to reach him better. Leaning onto him, he held me as we kissed and kissed.

My glasses went askew. Our clothes were too bulky to get a proper feel, and yet I craved his hands all over. He must have been feeling the same way, because one of his hands started its way down to the back of my jeans... but he stopped.

He pulled back from the kiss. "Let me take you home, before I do more here in the middle of the road."

"I can't do more. Not tonight."

He nodded and let me go. His arms still surrounded me, but he didn't hold me tight to him anymore. I fixed my glasses.

He searched my eyes. "If you still want to kiss me next time we meet, when you're not half-way drunk, then..."

"I said I wouldn't do this."

"I thought I didn't want it." His lips tilted in an ironic smile. "To be honest, I'm not sure what this means or where it'll go, but I can't say that I'm upset about it, after that kiss."

"Maybe it's a Christmas miracle— or karma. That, or the ghost of seasons past is haunting us."

"Let them. I'm not scared."

December 20

Daniel

LESS THAN A WEEK left before Christmas, and it was finally time for the last outside event. With the car parade about to start, we only had the big community party at the hall left. In a few days, I'd be free from the committee forever.

Vehicles decorated with colorful strings of lights and painted cardboard lined up around a street corner, hidden from the horde around the square. The onlookers packed both sides of the road, waiting to see the display; there were probably four times as many people as we'd had for the cookie competition. A speaker blasted music for everyone to enjoy, with a mix of merengue, salsa, rock and pop Latino, and rock classics from the US and the UK.

I moved through the line of cars, talking to the teams and making sure everything was in order. The procession would start with the elementary school submission and end with the volunteer one. Our decorated vehicle would carry Santa and wouldn't get a score, but I ensured the volunteer team was happy with it regardless. After double checking everything was set up to go right on time, I left them all idling and waiting for seven p.m. to hit.

Night had fallen a while ago and it grew cold fast. I made my way through the people waiting for the show; everyone wore thick jackets and chatted with each other. Several of them waved at me or said hi, completely ignoring the fact I didn't smile back and only nodded. Perhaps that was the real holiday spirit. They accepted me as I was. Something told me it would last throughout the new year, too. It wouldn't be exclusive to the season.

I reached the jury platform, placed next to the community hall entrance in front of the tree. My eyes found Ale as if drawn by her magnetism. A now-familiar flutter took over my stomach; I hadn't stopped thinking about our kiss two days before. We'd been too busy putting out fires for the groups participating in the car decoration competition to spend any time together, much less getting to chat about anything significant. In other words, I hadn't had a chance to gauge whether she still wanted to kiss me. I knew I wanted to kiss her, despite the persistent hesitation about it leading anywhere.

Several people gathered around the jury platform, a confusing cluster at the center. I elbowed my way into it as politely as I could.

"What's going on?" I asked.

Ale stood at the center of the cluster, holding Renata, and trying to help her sit on a cushioned armchair. Without giving it much thought, I joined and helped Renata down.

"Where did this chair come from?" I asked.

"Home," Ale said.

"She insisted." Renata huffed. "She's coddling me."

"You need to be coddled, I've heard." I let Renata hold on to my arm and settle down.

Ale and I exchanged a look. Butterflies took flight again.

"Okay, I'm set." Renata frowned. "Stop smothering me."

Ale didn't stop; she wrapped Renata in a couple of blankets. I retreated and smiled down at them. They looked so alike and yet so different; beyond aesthetic differences with how they styled their hair and chose their clothing, or how much fuller Ale's face and body were, details set them apart. The way Ale's mouth quirked at the corner, and even a certain difference in energy. No wonder Renata had never drawn me the same way. They were their own people, of course, and there had never been a click with her.

"Sooo... Renata couldn't miss this event?" I crossed my arms.

"I'm right here," Renata complained.

Ale straightened and addressed me, anyway. "She was missing out on all the Christmas fun she so loves. If she couldn't come to the happy, I'd bring her to the happy."

Renata stared up at her sister. "To promptly ignore me and talk about me to someone in front of me. Wow. Just because he kissed you."

She mumbled the last few words, but it seemed both Ale and I had understood.

"I'm not ignoring you—" Ale stopped and gaped at her. "What?!"

"You were talking to Ximena on the phone when you came home that day. You said he'd kissed you and you couldn't tell me, so she'd have to get your drunk voice note instead."

"Fucking thin walls." Ale glared around us, as if to dare anyone to listen in on the conversation.

No one seemed to be paying attention to us, but I shared her sentiment. No one needed to know something happened, and that we may or may not be kissing in the near future.

"Who's Ximena?" I made my voice low.

"A friend from back in the city."

"Anyway," Renata interrupted. "When is the parade starting?"

Renata's presence freed Ale from her evaluation duties. We helped set up Janet and Pri with clipboards, making the three judges for the event. At seven sharp, the first car made it around the corner. The crowd roared.

I leaned into Ale. "Do you want to watch the show? Or... can we talk?"

She agreed, the quirk on her lips intensifying. I guided her down the platform with a hand on her back. The privacy of the community hall would work, and I unlocked it for us.

We didn't enter the darkened place too far; we stood by the double doors, enough light coming from outside through the glass to see each other clearly.

Ale leaned against the wall and watched me. She waited for me to make a move.

I arched an eyebrow. "So, who else did you tell we kissed?"

"No one. I wouldn't have even told my friend, if I hadn't been a bit drunk."

"I see. Why? Should I take that as a sign that you don't want a repeat?"

"Do *you* want a repeat?" She bit her lip.

It pulled from me. It made me want to kiss her now and talk later. Forget all my hesitation and get lost in how good it had felt.

Except relationships were messy and rarely worth the effort. A conversation was the only thing that could prevent a fuck up.

"You didn't answer my question, but I'll give you an out. It's okay if you regret it." I crossed my arms. "Disappointment won't kill me."

She pursed her lips to the side, a sparkle of humor in her eyes. "Good thing I didn't fool myself into thinking you would be romantic about this thing between us."

I took a step closer to her. "I thought a kiss in the middle of the street was kinda romantic. The only thing that would have made it better would have been fluffy snowflakes falling over us. Like in Christmas movies."

The morning after, people had seen the message written on the street and some chatter had spread around. All comments about our vandalism had been accompanied by shaking heads and lighthearted quips. As far as I knew, nobody pointed fingers our way.

"I didn't need the snowflakes," she said. "And I don't regret it."

"But...?" I got a bit closer.

She blinked up at me. "You said you didn't see anyone in your future."

"You said you wanted to be alone for a while." I braced my arm on the wall. It made me close enough to get into her space. The smallest of movements would make us touch. "Seems we are at an impasse."

People shouted at the other side of the door, but we remained alone. Cars and lights and music enthralled everyone else, but all I could see was Alejandra.

She tracked my face. A hand rested on my chest.

Her tongue peeked out as she wet her lips. "What are we going to do about that?"

"We should give it time. See if this... fades." I put a hand on her plush hip. I dug my fingertips into her flesh.

"I said I'm done with grumps." The hand she'd placed on my chest made a fist, wrinkling fabric among her fingers. Pulling me closer. "But I've been told I'm good with them."

"I thought this feeling would last a week at most. It's been more than a month, and it keeps on hanging on."

She stretched her neck and offered me her lips. I leaned closer but didn't kiss her yet.

"I think..." Her voice dropped to a murmur, the air of her words a caress against me. "I think we should test the waters. Take it slow."

I pressed my body against hers and trapped her against the wall. "Give it some time to see if we're wrong..."

"Or if there's a reason grumps—"

I kissed her. I let myself take her mouth like we weren't taking it slow. It didn't even matter that I had no idea where she was going with her sentence; I didn't care. I planned to show her what *this* grump could do.

My heart beat fast. Blood rushed in my ears. I sought her tongue with mine, learning the way she wanted to kiss me.

She devoured my mouth. I moaned. Her body moved against mine, but I somehow knew she wasn't asking for space. She asked me for more. For touch.

I gave it to her. The hand on her hips explored paths over her body; places safe enough for the community hall. Places that kept me a gentleman, when she'd asked to take it slow.

There wasn't a lot I could do about the speed at which my cock got hard, so I pulled back... for now.

I took a deep breath. "People in Laguna Island won't get that this isn't a big deal. I'd rather we kept it private until we gather more evidence about where this is going."

"People here can be old-fashioned. I don't want them jumping to conclusions when I just moved back. That's fine by me."

We didn't say much more than that. We kissed again, and soon she knew all too well what it did to me. She didn't seem to mind, the way she rubbed against me.

It took some time for the crowd outside to dissipate. We stayed in the privacy of the hall for as long as we could, making truth out of our words.

December 22

TWO DAYS AFTER THE car competition and two days before the big party, the last meeting of the season was all hands on deck. The core six volunteers plus several others gathered at the hall, intent on finalizing every tiny detail.

While I focused on stringing together garlands, Daniel moved from group to group with his clipboard. A serious look on his face, he went about solving problems, keeping people to task, and stealing glances in my direction. After a while, I lost count of how many times I caught him gazing at me from afar.

It was easy to forget we were keeping it quiet when I held his gaze across the room. My fingers stilled, a forgotten red ribbon bow in my hand. We'd stolen a couple of frenzied moments since our first make out session and had done lots of kissing each time. Some exploring. A few tentative questions about what it all meant.

The memory of his whispered words as his hands wandered more and more weakened my knees. It melded with my reaction to him cutting down that tree, imagining him going at me with that intensity... that power...

"Ahem— We ran out of tape." Janet blinked at me. I wasn't sure whether she simply wanted me to solve the problem for her, or she was letting me know I was being way too obvious.

I stared at her for a few seconds, crossing my fingers my wits would come back online.

"Uhm...what about..." I rummaged on the table. "This! Staple it."

"Sure." She took the stapler from me and smirked. "But we're still going to need tape."

"Mh-hm, mh-hm. Okay. I'll go check—"

"Hey." Daniel interrupted me but, somehow, I didn't mind. "I need to talk to you. In private. Co-chair stuff."

The little smile on Janet's face intensified. I could practically hear the assumptions going off in her mind.

I ignored her and turned to Daniel. "I'm on my way to the storage room to check for extra tape."

"We'll pretend it's our office, then." He placed a hand at the small of my back and guided me out.

The storage room had enough space for shelves on every wall, full of serviceable knickknacks, toilet paper, and office supplies. It also had a door and a lock, which Daniel closed thoroughly. The click of it resounded on the space, highlighting the reduced dimensions of the room.

"Fuck, I need a break." He rested against the door and sighed. "Too much socializing."

"I'm going to assume that's why you locked us in? So no one bothers us?"

"Sure." He pushed himself off the wooden surface and prowled toward me. "That's why."

"I can't fathom any other reasons." I smirked.

His voice turned into a rumble. "Then I'm not doing things right."

He grabbed me by the nape and pulled me to him. His lips immediately intense, he kissed me like he craved me. Like he couldn't get enough of me. I grabbed his blue plaid shirt in both hands; my knees wobbled. I needed support.

With the full weight of his body, he pressed on me until I hit a shelf. Metal dug into my shoulders and lower back, yet I didn't care. I unbuttoned his plaid and ran my hands over his undershirt.

He kissed my jaw, my neck. "I've been thinking about this."

"Me too."

"How much?" He nibbled on my clavicle.

I grabbed him by his belt and pulled him closer to me. "Lots. So much."

"What have you been thinking about? Be specific."

"Your cologne."

He grabbed the rolls above my jeans, his teeth on my earlobe.

"How your plaid shirt always reminds me of you chopping down that tree."

He chuckled. "Think about that much?"

"Plenty brawny for me, yes."

His hands went around to grab handfuls of my ass. "Tell me more."

"Do you like it when I talk? Tell you what kind of horny thoughts you put in my mind?"

He groaned and kissed me so hard I almost forgot I'd asked him a question.

He pushed his erection on me. "Yes. I want to know every one of those thoughts."

"Well, then let me tell you—"

A knock at the door interrupted us. The frown that appeared on Daniel's face was the worst I'd ever seen.

Fuck, he uttered.

"So how about that tape?" Janet asked from the other side of the door, humor in her voice.

"She knows," I whispered. "Or she wouldn't have knocked."

Daniel groaned.

"Still looking!" I pushed Daniel away and straightened my clothes.

"We're still talking about confidential committee business." He added as he accommodated his hard on in his pants.

"Wonderful. A-ha." A snicker reached us from outside. "We'll be waiting. I'll tell them to use the glue sticks creatively. Oh! We ran out of staples, too. I'm going now."

"Wonderful indeed," I said to Daniel alone. "The rumour mill will officially start running now. How long did we keep it private? Two days. Only two days!"

He pursed his lips. "Let them talk about it then. They're not wrong and we can't stop it. Want to go with me for coffee? If we stay here, I'll want to go right back to it."

"We'll buy some tape on the way."

After six weeks working for the committee, stopping by Eva's coffee shop brought a familiar wave of coziness to me. Daniel opened the door and, as soon as we'd stepped inside rEvalution, Eva's hands began moving on her espresso machine.

"The usual?" She asked. "A large black and a cortado. We'll deal with payment in a sec."

"I can help if you like." I leaned across the counter to peek at her POS. "Yep. I'm familiar with this system."

Eva arched an eyebrow. "Oh? Sure. Show me."

I rounded the counter and set up behind the screen. I tapped a few buttons until I figured out where everything was.

"Okay, let's see... done." I blinked at Daniel. "It'll be six dollars, but make it ten to add a wonderful tip in thanks for letting me play barista."

Daniel smirked and paid.

Eva laughed. "Do you want to play barista? You seem to be my favorite kind, getting those extra tips."

"I worked as a barista during college. I liked it."

Eva gave us our coffee cups. "Do you know how to serve a good coffee?"

I went back to the patron side of the counter. "Yep. I don't think I'll ever be as fast as you, but I remember. I loved it."

"Are you looking for a job?"

I startled. Daniel and Eva stared at me, unwavering.

"Not really. Not until my sister's doing better. The committee has taken me away from her enough."

"What about some casual help? Just a few hours a week on my busiest times. Starting in the new year."

"I'm still not sure what I want to do in the long term..."

"Then it's a good idea." Daniel put a hand on my back. "Just to give you something to do. Get out of the house for the next few months."

"Think about it," Eva said. "I'll text you."

I nodded and we said goodbye.

We walked by the center fountain of the plaza when Daniel asked me about the party.

"Is Renata coming on Saturday?" he asked. "Do you need help? I can drive you both."

We made arrangements and, at some point during our walk, we'd started holding hands. If the chisme was about to make its way through the town, then we'd do it on purpose. We may not have decided yet where this would go, but we didn't need to hide.

Daniel may be cranky, but we clicked. He was the kind of man my ex never was; I already knew Daniel was a reliable man. He had goals and pursued them relentlessly and, in those moments alone, he showed me a side of him that I wanted more of. He was just my type.

Maybe this thing could go somewhere. Maybe I wanted him to lead me to an actual relationship. Despite how much I'd resisted it.

Maybe I wasn't done with grumps, after all.

Shit.

December 23

Daniel

I WALKED OUT OF my office and into the night, after catching up with my typical workload. The party was set and ready for the next day and, so far, no new fires had interrupted my usual tasks.

This time of the day was typically my favorite. It was full of possibilities: did I want to go eat at the pub? Go visit with Eva and discuss how we could improve the town? Go home, cook, and read for the evening?

The answer came to me, crystal clear. I wanted to spend time with Alejandra.

No other visions accompanied it. Almost like it didn't matter to me how we spent the evening, I craved her company. But she'd texted me in the morning to say she would spend the day with Ren, so I couldn't do that.

I let my feet take me to rEvalution instead. It was only half-an-hour until closing time, and a lonely patron left just as

I went in. The place was quiet now, except for Eva, who was cleaning up her workspace.

"Hey." I grabbed a duster Eva had left on the counter and took it to the shelves on the other side of the room. I spoke loud enough to be heard. "Closing up a few minutes early today?"

"Probably. I could use an early night."

"How about an actual vacation? I don't think you've taken time off since you opened this place last year."

"I'll go somewhere in the spring. Or fall. Depending on whether I can convince Ale to help me out here and how comfortable she gets running the show. Do you know what she'll end up doing in the long term? Aside from doing you, of course."

My lungs quaked and a forceful gust of air left me, halfway to a chuckle. "Wow. I gather you heard something."

"It's my job in our plans, isn't it? To keep my ears open for chatter around the town."

I made sure to move things around the shelves, cleaning around everything and organizing things into their place.

I ran the duster across the top trim. "Didn't know it would include keeping your ears open to rumors about my love life. But, no. I don't know what she wants to do in the long term, except help take care of Ren for the next few months."

"Love life, ah?"

I turned to her and crossed my arms, the duster hanging from my hand. "That's the part you focus on?"

She shrugged. "People think you two are cute. Leslie said she saw it coming from a mile away, the way you looked at her at the cookie competition. And the way Ale made you smile. You, the town's number one grump."

"Please." I scoffed. "I laugh. Once in a while."

"I don't think people knew that." A small smile appeared on her mouth.

She didn't look at me, but focused on wiping the counters.

I frowned. "You can erase that smile from your face. It's not a big deal."

"It isn't?"

"It is—"

I interrupted myself. Standing by the shelves at rEvalution, a limp duster in my hand, my brain short-circuited.

"It is," Eva repeated for me.

I sat on the armchair near me and grabbed the duster handle with both hands. "Oh, shit."

"Did you think this was a casual thing? Are you shocked?"

"I am shocked. Yes. Fuck." I rubbed my eyebrow with a hand. "I didn't want a relationship. They're too much effort."

"I agree with that, but since when are you afraid of working hard for what you want? You moved to Laguna Island knowing this would take years of perseverance. Why is a relationship different?"

She leaned on the counter, resting on her elbows and watching me carefully.

Eva waited for my answer. In all our conversations, we hadn't really gotten personal like this, but I had to admit it was a good thing. It forced me to find the answer inside, because even if this scared me, I was not a liar.

I held my friend's gaze. "Because I don't know if the effort is going to be worth it."

"How do you know the work you're doing for Laguna Island will result in what you want?"

"Because I won't let it be any other way."

"I think you can think of relationships that way, too. As long as you and everyone involved are on the same page, you can make it happen. The question is, do you want to commit to it the same way you committed to Laguna Island?"

"I think..." I stood and stared out the window. "I think I want to see where this goes. Put work into it, too."

"Then go tell her." Eva stretched a hand; I gave her the duster. "See if she wants that, too."

I smiled at her. "Thanks, Eva."

She didn't say anything else; she gestured toward the door to get me out into the night.

———

I parked outside of Ale and Ren's house and watched the windows like a creep. The curtains were closed and I couldn't see inside; not even shadows hinted at any movement in the home.

The worst stakeout ever could end with a simple text. I could send Ale a message and tell her I was outside, but I stalled. Mostly because I wanted to know what the hell to tell her, and I wasn't sure yet.

I leaned on the steering wheel and rested my head on my forearms. A slow and deliberate breath made it through my lips.

How to tell Ale that, after only a couple of days, I had changed my mind and wanted to see where our relationship could go? Maybe I could give it some more time and see if she might start feeling the same way.

Waiting seemed like a coward's solution. Could it be smart, too?

Maybe I should go home.

Or maybe I should just go talk to Ale and end this uncertainty.

A knock on the passenger window had me jumping in my seat.

Ale stood at the other side, a worried wrinkle on her eyebrow. "You okay?"

"Fuck." I lowered the window between us. "Hi."

"What are you doing here?"

"I was... I thought... I wanted to chat with you."

"Wow." She smirked. "I've never heard you unsure like this. Should I be worried? No— don't tell me. Did we lose Santa?"

"No, nothing like that. I just—wait. What are you doing out here?"

"I was locking the door and peeked out the window— saw the truck. Come, let's talk inside. I'm cold."

Without waiting for my answer, she went back into her place.

"No—" I stopped when she was too far away to possibly hear me. I raised the window and got out of my truck. "I was trying to be stealthy."

She waited for me by the door; I entered the home to find Ren sitting on the sofa in a blanket nest. It looked like Ale might have been sitting with her sister.

"And here I was," Ren said from her spot, "giving Ale grief for bringing her city ways home and locking the door."

The sisters' home looked cool, an old-yet-modern vibe that I could appreciate.

I didn't spend much time admiring the space, as Ren inspected me with a raised eyebrow.

"I wouldn't have seen him outside if it weren't for my city ways." Ale closed the door behind me and invited me to sit on the one armchair.

I shook my head. "I wasn't sure I was going to come knock at the door, or text you, or hell, figure out what window was yours and throw a few pebbles that way."

"Mmh." Ren squinted my way. "That makes me think you're not here to inquire after my health."

I shook my head again, but Ale was the one to answer.

"He wants to *talk*."

"No, no, no." Ren pointed a finger at the door behind me. "That sounds like code to having his way with you. We have thin walls, remember? Our beds share a wall, for heaven's sake. I'm not having you both *talking* in here."

"I think he actually meant talking, Ren—"

"I don't want to talk or *talk* here—" I crossed my arms.

Ren burrowed into her blankets and opened her book. "Go. Go somewhere and talk... or *talk*... or whatever."

"Are you sure?" Ale asked.

Ren sighed. "Yes, I'm sure. It's Christmas Eve Eve. Go be merry and find a reason for the season."

"Shut up." Ale laughed.

"Let's go to my place." I put a hand on Ale's back. "I haven't had dinner yet. We'll talk while I make something, then I'll bring you back."

"Or not," Ren said. "Depends on how merry you get, right?"

———

Ale

Daniel's small condo did not shock me in the least. Somehow, I fully expected the dark gray walls, broken by big prints framed in white, and a charcoal sofa in front of a big TV. An armchair in caramel leather plus a wooden center table gave the room warmth, and the mostly-white kitchen opened the space.

"Wow." I gave my jacket to Daniel, who hung it from bronze hooks by the door. "This is very modern and tasteful, and just what I imagined your place would look like."

He guided me to the sofa with a hand on my back. "I used to live the high-up-the-ladder corporate life. I got used to some comforts."

We sat in the small loveseat, side by side but angled towards each other. Daniel gazed at me with eyes that periodically narrowed, and lips that quirked randomly.

"You're thinking hard." I rested an elbow on the back of the sofa, my head in my hand. "Want to let it out?"

"No."

I laughed. "You're terrible. Then why bring me here?"

"To talk. But I wasn't sure I wanted to talk tonight, remember? You caught me parked outside your house and one thing led to another. Now we're here."

"Okay. Are you taking me home, then?"

"No. Let's talk."

"Oooh... kay." I settled deeper into my position, fully resting and watching him struggle.

"The thing is..."

"Uh-huh?"

"What I was thinking was..." He frowned. I pursed my lips not to smile. "Well..."

"Right, that makes sense." I nodded.

He glared at me. "Give me a sec to find my words, will you?"

"For sure, go ahead. Take your time."

He squinted at me, but the stare soon devolved into a sheepish gesture. Like he was unsure of himself. I'd only known him for six weeks, yet in all the time we'd spent together, I had never seen him nervous. Now, sitting in his apartment in the dim light of the entrance lamp, he showed me a new side of him.

A grump who felt anxious about telling me something.

A grump who'd invited me to his home, a space he never planned to share with anyone else.

A grump I had developed some new and promising feelings for.

"Oh... Ooohhh..." I straightened tall in my place, the excitement of the dots I'd connected filling me with potential energy. "You changed your mind!"

"What?"

"You're trying to tell me you want to be with me! Talk about a Christmas miracle. You figured out you feel something for me, too!"

"Ale— What—" He shook his head. "Wait. Did you say, *too*?"

"So frigging adorable for a grump. Ugh!" I shook my fisted hand between us. "The ghost of Christmas present is haunting you and showing you that the true meaning of the season is to let someone into your heart!"

The tiny smile that appeared on his lips seemed to pain him. "Stop."

"But the ghost of Christmas past is showing you that ooOOoOOoooh, it's scaaary to show your feelings..."

"Please. If you only let me put my thoughts together—"

By this point, my words came out breathless as I held back the cackling. "The question is, will the ghost of Christmas future show you a relationship between us? Only if you're brave enough to tell me how you feel!"

Humor broke his resistance and lit up his face. "Oh, shut up."

He jumped me. His lips clashed with mine in the same instant he pushed me back and landed on top of me.

I laughed, interrupting the kiss.

"Unbelievable. Attacking me with Christmas nonsense." He kissed my jaw.

"You were being so adorably nervous!"

"I'm pretty sure that's not what the ghosts did in that story."

I surrounded him with my arms and let him kiss my neck. My eyes closed. "I wouldn't know. I've never read the book or watched any of the movies."

"And I wasn't nervous."

"You were nervous!"

He nibbled on my clavicle. It was one of the moves he'd done on me as we made out, that I had quickly learned made me weak.

"I thought you were going to end things when you knew I changed my mind after only two days." He rested his weight on his elbows and gazed down at me. His eyes softened, the brown of them gentle. "I wasn't sure how to tell you that I want to work to make our relationship last. That as long as you keep on not taking my crankiness too seriously, I'll keep on finding ways to laugh with you."

The weight of him comforted me, heavy like a calming blanket. Yet lightness filled up my chest at his words; gravity itself couldn't hold me down.

His curls fell on his forehead. I ran my fingers through them, pulling his hair back.

"I like laughing with you. I like that I can do that."

"Laugh with me, then. Tell me I'm the worst and make a joke. But when we can't find joy, let us work through it and come out happy at the other side."

"I see." I pulled a face. "The message of the season got into you. It's all about joy now."

"How dare you?" He poked my side. "All you had to do was say yes. Say yes." He poked me again.

"Yes to what? I'm never saying yes to the Holiday spirit."

"Fuck's sake, Ale. Say yes to being with me. We can be cranky together, then laugh about it. Because with you, I want to."

"I'm not cranky!"

He poked. "Say yes."

His hand massaged the spot where he'd dug his finger. In a swift move, he found the edge of my shirt and caressed his way up my waist. The warmth of his hand immediately soothed my skin.

"I think you should tell me about your feelings some more." I ran my fingers down his sides and followed his lead; I pushed his clothing out of the way and touched him, my hands going up his back as far up as I could.

"I want to be alone— with you." He squirmed on top of me, his weight still on the one elbow. Our clothes loosened up between us, giving us access to explore further. Soft stomach to soft stomach, our hands surveyed new territories. "I want to put work into a relationship, if it's with you. Happy? Now say yes."

His eyes remained serious, intense as always, focused on me. The hand traveling on my skin wrapped around my ribcage, fingers splayed and expansive. His thumb caressed the underside of my breast, over the lace of my bra.

I loved that he wanted to hear my yes. That he was a grump who wanted to be with me, laugh with me, work at things with me.

His question was all about committing to each other. Having always shown me he was the reliable kind, Daniel made it easier to say yes.

My insides melted, warm wax softening into the coziest feeling. I was still done with exasperated, attractive men, but not for the same reason as two months earlier. This time, it was because I had found the one true grouch for me.

"I'm positively merry." I smiled and let my hand wrap around the soft flesh above his belt. I squeezed. "And yes. I want that, too."

He returned my grin and kissed me again, hard. "I thought so, but are you always going to make me work like this?"

I hooked a leg behind his. "I think so, yes."

He shook his head. His hand traveled up and down my waist, waking up my nerve endings, until it settled on the soft rounds of my hips.

"Mmmh. Good thing I'm not afraid of hard work." He got up and pulled me up from the sofa. "Come. I'm hungry."

He'd given me no warning and I got up too fast— a dizzy spell struck me.

I leaned on him. "Wait— what? You're going to cook now?"

"I want dessert first." He turned me with two firm hands on my hips and pushed me toward a short hallway.

"Oh. Oooh. I see. You're decisive like this, and now that we made up our mind..."

His room was a decent size, with a big window overlooking a small park, a king-size bed, and a wall-to-wall closet with several doors, some of them open. Dark gray covered the walls here again, but all the furniture and even the duvet were white, helping brighten the space. A patterned geometrical blanket in yellow, earthy tones covered the foot of the bed. He guided me all the way to it, at the side of the bed, before he turned me back around to face him.

"Unless you still want to take it slow, in which case we'll go out and get a sandwich from the damn gas station, to avoid temptation."

He took his hands off me as he waited for my answer, as if even the simplest touch would urge him forward. My face took on the comfortable, familiar shape of a smirk.

I hooked my index finger on his belt and pulled him to me, until his body and mine touched from chest to toes. "I can't wait to see what this brawny lumberjack can do with me."

A cheeky smile tilted his lips upward. His hands settled on my hips again. "And to think I almost tried to escape you and go chop that tree alone."

I unbuttoned his plaid shirt. "I almost want you to keep this on."

"I can do that. You keep your glasses on, okay?"

"Okay." I dropped my hands do this belt. "Anything else?"

He let me take his belt off, a satisfying *whoosh* as it rushed through denim hoops. He stopped me when I tried to unbutton his jeans.

With a gentle caress, he ran his hands down my arms and to my hands. He held them and gave me a soft kiss, only to change the tone by lifting my arms above my head.

A shiver ran through me. He smiled. With firm hands, he grabbed the hem of my top and pulled it off me in one swift move.

My hands dropped to his shoulders as his eyes devoured my chest.

"Ugh." His eyebrows furrowed. His hands wrapped my breasts, testing the weight of them. It seemed to pain him. "What a lovely color. The yellow is perfect against you. With all the black you wear, surprise colors are a gift. And a nagging question in my mind all the time. What color will you wear next?"

Need for his hands all over me took over, a steady increase of my heartbeat drumming against my breastbone.

I grabbed the bottom of his plaid and undershirt and pulled up. "I changed my mind. I want your skin against mine."

He let me take off his shirts and rub myself on him. The hairs of his chest tickled me. The softness of his small tummy and his thick arms around me gave me confidence. He was bigger than me. Stronger. He could take me.

His hands grabbed handfuls of my ass. "Give me the benefit of the doubt, okay? If I'm weak in the knees— hell, if I fucking faint— it's because I haven't eaten since lunch."

"Not because you're so overcome by how much you want me?"

"Maybe that, too." He smiled. "Now, let me get to know your body."

"Mmmh. Where should we start?"

He traced the lace trim of my bra, his eyes following the tips of his fingers. His thumbs circled my nipples through the cloth.

"Let's take this beautiful yellow bra off. I want your tits in my hands. My mouth."

He helped me unhook the piece of clothing and get rid of it. He filled his hands with my full breasts as I dropped my bra on the floor.

He groaned. "Yes. So good."

One small, insistent step at a time, he pushed me to the edge of the bed. I busied myself unbuttoning his jeans and pulling them down his narrow hips; he held me by the shoulders and pushed me onto the bed. I scrambled back on it, wearing nothing but my panties, while he got rid of his jeans and socks.

He crawled to me, his eyes ravishing me. "I want to take my time with you."

"You might starve."

"It would be a good death. My mouth full of you."

"I like it rough, Daniel."

"You do, huh?" He settled between my legs, and promptly dug his nose in my neck. "I can be rough."

"Will you make me beg?" My breathing quickened. "From your flirting I thought you'd be into it."

"I'll want to make you beg at times, yes." He switched sides and nibbled on my earlobe, as his hand found my breast and kneaded it an exploring rhythm. "But we'll see what we come up with today."

Both our hands explored everything within our reach. My hands traveled over his neck, and my fingers got lost in his hair. His hands grabbed onto the plush, round lines of my body, on my waist and hips. I held on to the curves that overflowed the elastic of his boxers; he gripped handfuls of my thick thighs.

Our breaths mixed as we kissed. I undulated my body beneath him, craving his weight on me, and his skin rubbing against mine. He pushed on me, the padding around his body not enough to soften his strength, or the hard lines of his muscles and bones. It made me delirious with the blooming sensations all over my body.

His mouth closed over my nipple; he played with the other between his fingers. It sent shivers through me and I dissolved further into the mattress. My head fell to the side. I would have closed my eyes, except I caught a flash of movement— there were mirrors behind the open closet doors, and I could see our reflection there.

"Oh, fuck." I watched my fingers disappear in the curls of his hair, his eyes closed as he played with my nipple in his mouth. "Fuck, yes."

Something about my tone must have drawn his attention. He stared at me, then followed my gaze to the mirrors.

A slow, wolfish smile took over his lips. "Oh, I see. That's an idea."

He got up, his erection big and straining against his black boxers. He opened the closet doors further, all the way back against the shelves, so they formed a two-panel wall of mirrors. He stood back to check the results.

"Can you see your whole body?" he asked.

"Yes. I want to see what you'll do to me."

He groaned. "Deal. But first..." He dug around in one of the open shelves in his closet, looking for something— after a moment, he came out with a closed box of condoms he threw to the head of the bed. "You're staying the night, right?"

"Right. I see what you meant by taking your time."

"Uh-huh. So... will you stay?"

I bit my lip. "Yes."

"Good. Now, where were we?" He wasted no time climbing on top of me again. "Yeah, this."

He grabbed my breast in his hand, holding it firm. My nipple stood out, brown and pebbled. We both stared at it in the mirror, before Daniel licked it deliberately. His soft, pink tongue lapped at it. I moaned.

"I could get used to this." He sucked my nipple into his mouth. His reflection looked focused, intent.

"I wouldn't get to see this without those mirrors. I didn't know I'd like a new point of view this much."

"Let's see what else we like."

He took turns with my breasts, my neck, until all I wanted to do was close my eyes and get lost in the sensation. But I would open my eyes and melt all over again, at the way he seemed to focus on me, my skin, and get pleasure out of it.

He rubbed his erection on my sex. "What else shall we do, Ale?"

"I can't think." The words came out tremulous out of my throat. "Do you have ideas?"

"I planned a few things as I sucked on your nipples. Want to hear it?"

"No. Show me."

"Even better."

He sat on the edge of the bed and guided me to sit on his lap. My body was so soft that he had to help me, and I had to lean on him. My back to his torso, he placed my legs on top of his, my feet hanging on the outside. It opened my knees wider than his, held in place by his thighs.

I was on display in front of the mirrors.

"Do you have any idea how hot you look?" he asked.

Our reflection mesmerized me. His eyes surveyed the mirror, catching details of the image of us just like I did. His eyes sparkled, telling me I wasn't alone in enjoying every little aspect of it.

His fingers traced the curves of my supple flesh melding to his thighs, soft dough to his hard lines. One of his hands traced the crotch of my panties, while the other held on to my belly.

My mouth opened, jaw slack, as I labored to get more oxygen into my overworking lungs. Daniel's eyes caught on my breasts, and the hand that had been on my belly lifted to my chest. He cupped me, his thumb flicking the hard nipple.

"Fuck. Magnificent. Do you see this?" He massaged my breast. He seemed unable to tear his eyes or hands off my body.

I didn't want him to. I wanted his hands all over. And my turned-on face, with faint color on my cheeks and bright eyes, showcased it to both of us.

"Look at this now." He dug two fingers under the crotch of my panties, and explored the soft flesh, teasing.

My moan came from so deep in my chest that I hiccupped. He pushed the two fingertips into my slit, found my clit, and pressed on it. I jerked against him.

"Fuck." His other hand abandoned my chest and pulled the strip of fabric to the side. The view of his fingers playing on me was clear on the mirror. An intensely focused frown wrinkled his forehead, his head resting on my shoulder and intent on the image being reflected at us. "This is fucking brilliant. Look at your face. Look at your pussy. Those tits. Incredible."

He pushed those two fingers into me and my whole body quivered. Seeing his fingers disappear into me, the angles of his arm and wrist sharp to get as deep as he could, had my breathing turning into gasps.

He pumped his fingers a couple of times, tendons straining. A strangled noise left him.

"Come on." He removed his hands from my crotch and slapped my thigh. "Get up. In front of me."

I did but barely. He held me by the hips for the second it took to find my balance. As soon as I was stable on my feet, he pulled my panties down.

"Yeah. Stand naked like that. Let me watch you." He pulled me back close to him, between his legs. The same focused frown and intense eyes decorated his face, his head right around the plump lines of my waist. "Feet wider."

His hand guided my legs apart from the back. His fingers traveled up to my sex, his index making a soft pass from the front of my slit to my entrance. I moaned; he pushed the two middle fingers inside of me.

"I think that clit needs some love, don't you?" he asked, his voice grumbly. His index finger played with the swollen nub. "Mmh. You're getting soaked."

"You're taking this too slow." The words barely made out through my panting. "I need more."

He removed his hand from me again and ignored the accompanying moan I let out. He stood behind me and took off his boxers. "Fine. But just wait until I eat something. After a good, hearty snack, I shall have you gagging for it."

"Promises, promises."

"You'll see." He threw the remaining piece of fabric to the floor, then manhandled me back to the bed. "You expected me to want to make you beg. I'll show you what that means."

He positioned me at the feet of the mattress facing slightly away from the mirrors. With one firm hand, he guided me to put one knee on the bed, keep the other foot on the ground, and pushed my torso down into a doggy position.

I had to twist at the waist to see myself in the mirror, but I braced myself with my elbows. He checked the reflection, and angled my hips to show my ass as much as possible while keeping my torso visible as well.

He wrapped his cock in his hand and pumped several times, his eyes fixed on my pussy. "You're going to taste so good on my tongue. I know it."

"Then get on with it," I whined.

"Yes, ma'am."

He knelt behind me and buried his face in my tender flesh. He sucked on my clit and teased it with the tip of his tongue; I clung to the pretty blanket beneath me. Tremors ran through my body, building pleasure inside of me. He moaned against me and he fisted his cock again, teasing himself as he ate me out. Every detail was visible to me.

With his free hand, he parted my lips wide and lapped, then pushed his nose onto my clit.

"This is what I meant." My breath hitched. "So good."

"I want so much more. Hours of this with you." He continued to work me hard, while his hand kept a slow rhythm on himself. He used his fingers on me while he stole a good look at us in the mirror. "Yeah. So much more of this. Can't get enough of looking at you like this."

My skin felt hot all over, and I was pretty sure all my blood filled out my lower belly and the full body of my clit. My muscles had begun to clench randomly, chasing my climax.

"Do I taste as good as you thought?"

"Better." He licked again, overstimulating me. My nerves were on fire.

"Eat me out good, Daniel. Then I want to see you disappearing into me."

"Fuck." His fingers went knuckle deep into me. I whimpered. "Squeeze for me, Ale."

I did, letting my body clench at the edge of losing myself.

"Not going to be fucking enough." He removed his fingers and stood. "It's going to feel amazing around my thick cock. You see how hard I am?"

I nodded and licked my lips.

"I'm going to stretch you and fuck you so deep, I'm going to feel every one of your muscles gripping around me hard." He slapped my ass. "Don't come until I'm inside of you."

He lunged for the box of condoms. In his hurry, he tore it apart and the packets flew around us; a few landed on the bed and others on the floor. He threw the remnants of the cardboard package aside and picked a condom from the bed. He wasted no time rolling it onto his cock.

"Get to it, then." I snaked an arm underneath me and played with my clit and labia myself. I opened myself to him.

He stood behind me and admired the view for a moment. His cock stood thick and straight and imposing, but he wrapped it in a hand anyway. He got close enough to slap me with it a few times, before sliding the head up my slit and pushing the very tip of it into my entrance.

Our eyes locked in the mirror.

"Watch my cock disappear into you, Ale." One of his hands grabbed the flesh at my hip I couldn't see in the reflection, while the other moved my leg forward on the floor. It opened me wider for him.

I grabbed his balls and gently pulled him closer. "Get in me."

"Holy shit. Those nails are sharp, woman."

"Then you'll be careful until I tell you to fuck me hard."

"Guide me in."

I pulled again and he entered me slow. He whined and grabbed the rounds of my hips. I could only see his profile on the mirror— it looked pained— and my eyes wanted to close, but I made myself watch as every inch made it into me.

The first full stretch was my favorite part. Getting to see every detail of it had my heart beating as fast as it ever had. I moaned when he sheathed himself deep.

"Fuck, Ale." He ground his hips against mine. "You literally have me by my balls here. Let me do more."

My muscles tightened around him, the coiling tight in my lower belly.

"Ale." He slapped my ass again. His cock throbbed inside of me. "Play with your clit as I fuck you hard."

"Don't move yet." I let go of his balls and rubbed on my clit a few times. With index and middle finger, I teased the point where my flesh extended around him.

He groaned. "Please."

"Now who's begging?"

"I'll beg you. Let me fuck you hard. This is torment."

I burned. The way my body prickled, I'd come as soon as we got into it.

"Please. Please," he added. "I'm going to lose it."

"Don't move." I leaned forward, releasing half of his cock, before I pushed back and got him deep inside of me again. I moaned and repeated the motion a few more times.

He whimpered. "Holy... Christmas... ghosts."

A weak chuckle built in my throat, but it was overpowered by the fire roaring through me.

"I'm gonna come fast." I quickened the pace at which I pulled away and pushed back.

"Good. I'm not going to last either."

"Fuck me hard now. I want to hear you straining like when you chopped down that damn tree."

"Fucking finally." His fingers dug into my rolls harder. "Now don't *you* move."

I couldn't have done it if I tried. His hands gripped me hard as he went wild. My flesh, dark red-brown and swollen, responded to his thrusts, slam after slam of his hips against my ass. I braced myself with an arm on the mattress, doing my best to keep up with the strength of his pumping movements. With my free hand, I tapped lightly on my clit— anymore and I'd finish at once.

"You're so slick." He huffed, a strained sound I hadn't been able to forget in the weeks since I had first heard it. "So warm and tight around me."

"Tell me you're close."

"I'm close." He groaned. "Really close."

I arched my back to get him even deeper; the head lightly bumped against my cervix with each drive of his hips. The pressure shocked me— in a good way. It built further into my body and my mind went blank. I barely registered that I rubbed my fingertips on the head of my clit; the ensuing explosion triggered deep core convulsions that jerked each muscle through my body. I blissed out.

"Holy— damn— on earth—" Daniel whimpered.

His incoherent words brought me back. I'd fallen on my chest, the hand that had worked on my clit limp, and his continuing thrusts rocked my body. I had inadvertently closed my eyes, but now I could see my dreamy face, my skewed glasses, and the twitch of my thigh.

He half-held me up, fingers digging hard into my hips— I'd probably have bruises, but worth it— so I wouldn't fall. I firmed up the leg keeping me up again.

He slapped my ass one more time. "Good girl. Now I'm going to ride you right till I come."

I smiled. He closed his eyes, the worst frown I'd ever seen on his face, and pounded into me. His movements were frantic, desperate for his own orgasm. The pillowing expanses of my skin trembled with each one of his thrusts.

I twisted from my waist, my arm long towards him. I ran my sharp nails down his chest.

He bucked and fused into me, his ass tight as he pushed deep and released his load.

For a few moments, all I could hear was his rasping breaths and my slowing ones.

"I'm... seeing... white." He rested his weight on my hips. "Did I die?"

"That, or it's a Christmas miracle and it's snowing all around us." I leaned forward and rolled onto the bed. I took a deep, recovering breath.

He stumbled in his place and reached for the closet for balance. "A white Christmas is a statistical rarity in this section of the world."

"Oh, there you are. You're back, Mr. Grumpypants."

"Barely." He opened a single eye into a small slit. "Don't ask me to sign any documents or keep any coherent conversations."

"But you'll use big boy words, I see."

He smirked, both eyes sleepy but open now. He slapped my thigh in a friendly way before stepping out into the bathroom to dispose of the condom. Less than a minute later, he returned and joined me on the bed.

He cuddled right next to me, a hand over my waist and his nose in my hair. "Now I'm truly starving."

"For food?"

"I need a big dinner now. After a nap, maybe."

"A nap at this time is a terrible idea."

"I need to recover some energy before we do it all over again before sleep. And tomorrow morning before I take you home."

I caressed his arm on my belly. "For someone who planned to be alone forever, you really have a craving, don't you?"

"Did you see that the box of condoms was closed? I bought that when I moved here, just in case. Fuck yeah, I had a craving. A nutritional deficiency, at this point."

I laughed. "I got dick a couple of months ago and yet, I have to say I'd love to have more of what you're offering."

He scoffed and shook the handful of flesh under his hand. I chuckled.

"Unbelievable." His dry tone made me chuckle. "I suppose I'll give you more, now that we're going to let this thing between us persist."

"Sex is the holiday gift that will keep on giving."

"Maybe we'll have feelings about it one day, too."

"Maybe. We'll see where we're at next year."

"So frigging cheeky."

"So utterly cranky."

He shrugged. "You like me. It'll be fine."

"I suppose I do."

"You do. We'll be fine. We're good. It'll be worth it."

"We'll make it the best."

December 24

Daniel

THE COMMUNITY HALL BUSTLED with energy, the big Christmas party in full swing.

I strode through groups of people chatting with each other, and I avoided the children running around screaming. I'd taken Ale home in the morning after a night where we stayed awake more than we slept. She texted me earlier to say she was sore and would take a nap; it put a tiny curl in my lips I was sure she would call a smile.

I'd probably never admit it, but the not-a-grin gesture on my face was rooted in what some might call joy. Not for the season, but for the months ahead. Maybe years. The way I felt, it was easy to imagine this could last forever.

My eyes sought her in the crowd, a flutter in my belly. We'd agreed we'd find each other for the event, before we addressed the volunteers to thank them. Especially those on cleaning duty.

Ale and I? We were free after tonight. What a gift.

Someone patted my back in hello; Hana told me she'd round up the volunteers. I nodded a greeting back and continued my exploration through the hall. The decorations livened up the place, garlands of tree branches, red ribbons, Christmas symbols and decorations, and a million colorful tree lights entwined with them on the walls. A side table full of drinks and snacks kept people's energy up, as we all killed time in that window between dinner and midnight.

The Latine influence in Laguna Island helped explain why most people celebrated Christmas on the 24th, and why the party was held in between dinner and the time Santa delivered everyone's gifts to their homes. The party also served as an excuse for the kids to be outside of the house, giving their caregivers a chance to put their wrapped toys under the tree.

My mom hadn't held on to much of her culture, except for that. Gifts appeared magically under the tree right around midnight, while I went outside with my dad to look for Santa up in the sky. An actual smile curled my lips at the memory. Pity that consumerism had ruined everything.

Talking about Christmas traditions and other ailments...

I frowned. Ale didn't seem to be at the hall yet. I stood and turned in place, a full 360 degrees in search of her. I hadn't completed a quarter of it when someone attacked me via hat on my head.

"What?" I jerked and glared over my shoulder, to find a grinning blur of brown, pink, and orange hair.

"Hello, Santa." She kissed me. "So nice to see you."

"If this is what I think it is," I said as I pointed an accusatory finger at my head, "then how dare you?"

She laughed and gave me a quick peck on the lips. "You look cute in red, Mr. Grumpypants."

I squinted at her. I tried to get rid of the Santa hat. "Unbelievable."

"No! Don't take it off. Humor me for tonight."

"This goes beyond what I expected as reasonable relationship compromise."

She grinned, her eyes sparkling. "So what? You're not gonna give up on us now, are you?"

"Before we even really begin? Nah, you're stuck with me now. But you're lucky I like you this much."

With a flirty wink, she turned, grabbed my hand, and pulled me away.

A child stared at me.

"Boo," I said.

"Daniel!" Ale scolded me without even looking in my direction.

"What?" I said, before taking the hat off, stuffing it in my pocket, and following Ale to wherever she wanted to take me.

"Don't scare the children. Honestly."

"Where are you taking me?"

"You'll see."

She stopped by a non-descript spot by the wall. I gazed around but no one seemed to be paying attention to us, all uninterested in what we were up to.

I arched an eyebrow at her.

She smiled. "I'd estimate that eighty percent of Christmas symbolism was stolen from Pagans."

I tried to fight it but I lost— I smirked. "Sure. What are your references?"

"Just a gut feeling, but I'm confident. It's also not the point."

"What's the point?"

"The date in which we celebrate Christmas was also kind of stolen from the Pagans."

"Kind of?"

"Uh-huh. Yuletide is a big deal, and we may have accidentally been part of its magic."

I squinted at her. "What's going on?"

She pointed up with her index finger. A twig of mistletoe hung above us. I wanted to frown, pretend exasperation, but with her I couldn't.

"Mistletoe is considered deeply magical by some folk," she said.

"We're not in ancient Europe, Ale. Over here it's a pest." Despite my complaint, I stepped closer to her and put my hands on her waist.

"And yet. And yet! Our first kiss was under the mistletoe. What if it's a blessing to our relationship? I'd like to think it is."

I shook my head. "Believe in magic all you want, but I don't need that to believe in us."

"Believe in magic a little bit, because it's either that or holiday romcoms have more truth to them than I'm comfortable admitting to."

I gave her a soft kiss. "I'd rather we remain cynical of those, but I like what I'm hearing. That you're happy enough about us that you're ready to believe in the magic of the season."

"Not *of the season*— just magic. Magic in general, throughout the year. Catch me celebrating Beltane next."

I laughed, kissed her again, then pulled her away. "Come on, my little witch. I kissed you again under the mistletoe. Now we'll go talk to the volunteers."

"And next?"

"Next we'll learn more about those pagan holidays and make magic all year round."

Valentine's Day

Ale

AT THE END OF January, I'd started taking random shifts with Eva at her coffee shop. As Ren recovered further, she'd started to come with me; my twin sister would sit on the sofa, drink enormous amounts of coffee, and read. At least, that's what she did when she didn't end up talking with townspeople, or her friend Pri when she came from the library for a hot drink run and end up sitting around for lunch.

It made me happy to see my sister getting color back in her skin, and some weight back on her bones.

On my end of things, returning to the coffee-working field felt good. Now that I'd taken a break from my job in accounting, I didn't think I wanted to go back. Depending on Ren's recovery and how much I liked it at rEvalution, maybe I'd offer my freelancing services to Eva. We'd see. For now, she and I prepared for her to take some time off, before her trip to Vegas in May. I would keep the shop running for her while she took a solo weekend away. Between my love for the barista work and the extra cash, I enjoyed my current circumstances.

I would also have said that I was extremely happy about the state of my relationship with Daniel, except that on that fine Tuesday, February 14, he entered the shop with flowers, a chocolate box, and a red heart balloon.

I stared at him, frozen mid-counter wipe.

What the fuck? I uttered his way.

He must have been able to read my lips, because he gave me that small smile that had taken over his mouth, more often than not, when we were together.

Without any apparent shame, he sauntered to the counter where I remained frozen. He bent over the counter and gave me a hard, long kiss for a hello. I didn't move; I simply tracked him for signs of illness.

"Are you okay?" I asked.

He pushed all three things he carried my way.

"Happy Valentine's Day, Alejandra."

Ren's laugh, loud and joyful, reached me from the sofa.

"No." I shook my head. "Who are you, and what did you do to my boyfriend?"

"I can prove I'm the same Daniel you're in a relationship with. I have three words for you: magic, mirrors, and lumberjacks."

My cheeks warmed up. "What's wrong with you?"

"Don't you like to celebrate this date?"

"No! And I can't believe you would."

"Oh, I see." He leaned forward again, and called me closer to him with a beckoning finger. "Let me tell you."

I arched an eyebrow, but I gave him my ear.

"It's the one holiday where I get to do something most people would think is against my nature, with the perfect excuse to both do something nice for you and shock everyone into silence. Including you."

I was still processing his words when he took my chin with two firm fingers, aligned my face forward again, and dropped another kiss on me.

"I'll even drive you to dinner at a fancy restaurant tonight," he added. "And I'll tell you all about Lupercalia, which is likely the true origin of this celebration. Kind of secular, compared to Imbolc, and quite... cringy."

"You've got to be kidding me."

"C'mon," Ren said from her place on the sofa. Only as I drew my eyes to her, did I see our other patrons also enjoying the show. "Let the man show you some love."

I gazed around in search of support for me, but found none. Eva might have supported me, but she was busy in her office.

I threw the cleaning rag in its container under the counter and crossed my arms. I glared at Daniel. "We were meant to hate the holidays together. We bonded over our deep annoyance over Christmas! Now there's a celebration you're into? The one I least expected you to like? Valentine's Day isn't even a proper holiday!"

"It's full of consumerism, yes," he said, "and fake, mandatory declarations of love. But I wanted to join in the fun for this one."

"You are out of your mind. I don't know you."

His grin stretched wide and made the sense of betrayal slightly better.

"I have big feelings for you." He pulled on the string keeping the balloon secured, making it dance in the air. "Let me show you the one day I have the perfect excuse for it."

"People will talk about this. Too weird, corny, and out-of-character for you."

"Let them." He gave me another kiss. "What do I care? Totally worth it, if for your reaction alone. Seems I'm not the only grump in the relationship now, ah?"

"Is it my karma for not liking any holidays? That I'm in a relationship with someone who only likes the very worst of them?"

"No, our karma is that we got together over Christmas, so now the date will always have to be special to us. Now. Can I have my usual? I'll get to know Ren better while you finish your shift."

"Unbelievable. Truly the worst," I said, but a smile curled my lips regardless as I made him a drink, coffee as black as his soul.

I never expected this of my favorite grump, but ever since then, Valentine's was the one yearly date— aside from our birthdays— we celebrated.

Christmas never became a big deal for us. We gave each other a small anniversary gift but, otherwise, we kept it simple. Except for the fact we grumbled about it together, for every winter to come.

THE END

Would you like to read about their first Christmas together and learn why they have a Christmas tree in their home? Then visit
leonorsoliz.com/utm-2nd-ep,
join my newsletter, and receive the short story in your inbox!

Thank you

I HAD NEVER RUSHED to finish a story as I did with Under The Meh-stletoe. While I'm fortunate enough to have people in my life that I can rely on, I'm particularly thankful to them this time.

As always, I want to start by thanking my husband and our little family. Not only did Mr. Leonor come up with the title for this story, but he reassured me when I needed to be reassured, and edited within a short window of time so I could publish on time. Him and our child understood when I had to prioritize work on this story, and I don't take that lightly.

I also want to thank my online friends for their companionship. To every Discord server I'm in, thank you for your generosity and understanding.

Thank you to Sara, for helping me figure out solutions for my cover problems and being so fun to chat with. We'll go for coffee soon, I promise.

Thank you to Beth, for reading this quickly to let me know it wasn't trash. Also, you win the trophy for best gif use. I don't think you know how much I appreciate you and your gif game.

And a final thank you to my IRL friends, who encourage me every day to pursue my dreams.

About the Author

LEONOR WROTE HER FIRST Meet Cute at eight years old and never really stopped. After many years of practicing and dreaming, she took the plunge and wrote a full-length romance novel. Then she wrote some more.

Her stories are written for comfort: love as it can be. Writing love for today means diverse characters with emotional depth and wisdom. Her characters are doing the work, folks.

Leonor is a Latina living in Canada, working as a therapist during the day and fitting as much writing to her life as she can. She's also a multi-crafter, trying her hand at watercolor, jewelry, and anything else that strikes her fancy.

You can connect with me on:
www.leonorsoliz.com
hello@leonorsoliz.com
INSTAGRAM: https://www.instagram.com/leonor.soliz/
TIKTOK: https://www.tiktok.com/@leonor.soliz.author
FACEBOOK: https://www.facebook.com/leonorsolizz

Upcoming books by the Author

More in the Cozy Latine Billionaires series!

YOURS, FOREVER

Max and Eva. Marriage of convenience, what happens in Vegas...
comes back to haunt you.

YOURS, FINALLY

Jake and Vi. Brother's best friend and oh, so much pining.

YOURS, FOR GOOD

Javier and Nora. Daddy Long Legs retelling.

...And more Un-Merry Christmas is in the works, too!

check my plans at leonorsoliz.com/upcoming